SWEET VENGEANCE

SWEET DEMONS · BOOK ONE

VIANO ONIOMOH

SWEET VENGEANCE: Sweet Demons Book 1
Copyright © 2023 Viano Oniomoh
All rights reserved.

Cover, Interior Design, and Illustrations by Viano Oniomoh
designedbyvee.com

For more information, visit vianooniomoh.com

Published by Viano Oniomoh After Dark.

Paperback ISBN: 9798375809328
Hardcover ISBN: 9798375809489

Sweet Vengeance

SWEET DEMONS · BOOK ONE

To everyone dreaming of vengeance.

CONTENT NOTES

This book contains the following content that may be upsetting for some readers. For those who might need it, please scan the QR code below to take you to the page on my website where I list the content warnings.

If I've missed any warnings, please feel free to contact me and I will add them ASAP. Thank you!

Take care of yourselves!

With that, I hope you enjoy the story!

~Vee.

CONTENTS

ONE

Joy knelt in the middle of a circular rune drawn with white chalk, wearing nothing but a bathrobe. She'd thought she'd feel ill when she'd planned to do this; disgusted. She'd thought she'd be so overwhelmed with horrible memories it would leave her trembling with apprehension.

After what she only referred to in her head as "the incident", Joy had barely been able to look at herself. Taking off her clothes for any reason, even a fucking *shower*, had felt like a violation—and it was her own fucking body. Then, as time had passed, she'd slowly, *thankfully*, gone numb.

She'd thought the reality of what she was about to do would bring the disgust crawling back—would make her feel like peeling off her skin. But in the moment, it felt different.

No, it *was* different.

The difference was, this was her choice. She laughed, the sound short and bitter. Did demons even have sex? Did they have the appendages for it? Did they care for mortal, human women? Joy didn't know, and she didn't care.

If her body wasn't an acceptable sacrifice, and the demon said there was absolutely no other option, then Joy would just have to negotiate. She was an expert haggler—*thank you, Wuuye Market*—there had to be something the demon wanted other than a dead animal, because Joy was *not* about to sell her soul. No, she wanted to have her cake and eat it, too. Before she killed her rapist, she wanted him to suffer worse than he'd made her suffer, while she went on to live and thrive for the rest of her natural life. It would be the perfect conclusion to her perfect revenge.

She took a deep breath. There was another rune directly opposite and connected to hers, drawn this time in red chalk. It needed only one thing now to activate it.

For a moment, she hesitated. The morally upright Christian she'd been raised to be protested: *Isn't death too harsh a punishment for a rapist? For* any *criminal, for that matter?*

But the other side of her—the side that clawed for justice—for *vengeance*—screamed: *death is not enough.*

She picked up the kitchen knife and sliced a small cut quickly across her index finger. Blood spilled onto her circle, then the other. She sucked her finger into her mouth to stem the bleeding.

The room grew unbearably hot, sweat pooling in her armpits, between her breasts and thighs. The lines drawn in red chalk began to glow.

The demon appeared without fanfare—without a single rumble of thunder or the violent tremble of an earthquake. One moment, there'd been just the circle, and the next, they were there.

It felt like the room had shrunk about ten sizes under the sheer weight of their presence, all the air sucked into a vacuum.

The demon towered over her—they had to be at least seven and a half feet tall, and that was without the horns— with a broad, flat chest peeking out from dishevelled black robes that swept the floor. Said robes resembled shadows and smoke, rather than something solid. She could faintly make out fancy gold filigree designs along the cuffed sleeves and hems she swore on her life were *moving* as she stared. Hefty, ridged horns curved up and back from a mass of thick, coily locks, which fell gorgeously down their shoulders.

Their skin was just as dark as their horns and hair, and was hands down the most beautiful shade of plum Joy had ever seen; it was warm, smooth, and matte, making her recklessly want to reach out and touch. The phrase *"the darker the berry, the sweeter the juice"* ran through Joy's head before she could stop it, making her blush furiously. Sharp, pointed nails tipped their fingers, and their irises glowed in a thin ring of red, surrounding a large, black pupil she felt like she could drown in.

Something rustled, and Joy's eyes widened when the demon slightly spread their feathered wings, the dark appendages blending in seamlessly with their skin and robes.

Joy quickly rose from her knelt position, but it did nothing to lessen the intensity of the demon's domineering presence. In fact, standing as she was, the demon felt even taller, forcing her to tilt her head back to meet their eyes.

Her pulse raced madly; her breaths started to come fast. Joy wasn't a small woman in literally any sense of the word. She was six feet tall, and she was deliciously fat. It was a rare sight to find anyone bigger than her.

The demon seemed to be studying her as much as she was studying them, though nothing in their gaze gave their emotions away. Joy tugged her robe tighter around herself, self-conscious, as those red eyes trailed slowly from her bare feet, lingering on her exposed thighs, going all the way up to the short, trimmed afro on her head.

She suddenly felt painfully naked, but not in the way she'd expected. Her nipples stiffened at the intensity of their perusal, and to her horror, she could feel herself getting wet.

"Speak, human," the demon finally said, the deep timbre of their voice going straight to her cunt.

She pressed her legs together, clenching her jaw. Tried to remember what her aunt had told her.

"I'm here to make a deal," she said, thanking whatever gods existed that her voice came out firm and in control.

"That much is obvious," the demon replied tonelessly.

Her eyes narrowed. *The demon's got jokes*. Fantastic.

"You reek of bloodthirst," the demon continued, flicking their tongue out to wet the seam of their lips. Their tongue was a shocking, violent red, and was also *forked*. Holy Mary and Joseph. "You have summoned me to kill someone for you."

Joy's smile felt manic when she let her lips stretch with it. "No, *I* want to kill someone. I want *you* to make it look like an accident."

Desperation had brought Malachi here, to this gorgeous human with luminous dark brown skin and big, doe brown eyes blazing with a vicious, delicious hatred that made his skin sing.

They stood before him in nothing but a plain white bathrobe, glaring up at him almost defiantly. Despite their bravery, he could smell a hint of fear; the alluring, metallic tang of their spilled blood; and also a slight creamy sweetness he'd come to understand was the scent of a human's arousal.

The last scent discombobulated him, and had his own

body automatically trying to react. Why would they—? No, it made no sense at all. But they were standing in the sacrificial circle, did they mean to—?

No. He inwardly shook his head, and forced himself to concentrate on why he was here. Desmond's contract was going to end soon, and even though Malachi wouldn't exactly call them ... *friends*, Desmond was still Malachi's only source of sentient interaction he had outside of himself. And Malachi desperately didn't want to be alone.

There was also the fact that he was afraid Desmond's soul wouldn't be enough of a tether to keep him in the mortal realm. A tether via his contract was what had kept him here all this while, after all; he figured it was better to be safe than sorry.

"You haven't brought a sacrifice."

"I-I have." For a moment, the human's confidence faltered.

Their delicate hands played with the edges of their robe, then they abruptly tugged on the belt, loosening it, and let the robe fall.

And for the first time in his life, Malachi knew what it felt to properly feel desire; a pure carnal lust that snuck up on him like sentries in the night, stealing his breath and stiffening his dick.

Large, pretty drooping breasts with wide, dark areolas; big, curvy hips; a soft, rounded belly; and thick, luscious thighs with a thatch of curly dark hair at the apex. Lighter shades of brown slashed across their lower belly, under their arms, and across their thick hips like patches of lightning.

The longer Malachi stared, the more a trace of shame and anxiety bled into the human's scent.

Despite this, they still tilted their chin up high.

"I offer you my body," they said, their voice firm and sure.

Malachi didn't let any emotions show on his face. "And

what am I supposed to do with your body?" he forced
himself to ask, his voice coming out rough despite himself.

The human's shoulder jerked, too stiffly to come off
confident as they probably wanted. "Anything you want."
They swallowed visibly. "Just not … nothing that would
hurt."

Malachi paused, then took a step forward. The human's
throat bobbed with another swallow, but they didn't flinch
away.

For as long as the contract wasn't finalised, Malachi
couldn't leave the perimeters of his circle. But since they
were meant to be a sacrifice, he could reach into their circle
and touch them.

Should their skin have been burning to the touch, he
wondered, using the knuckle of his index finger to tilt their
face up even more, baring the vulnerable arch of their throat.
As they stared up at him, with those big, doe eyes, for a
moment, Malachi was seized with desperate temptation.

He thought of getting rid of his robes, and then getting
rid of theirs—of pressing their bodies together, simply to feel
the heat and solidity of another being for just one moment.
His skin felt overly sensitised in the moment, almost fevered
with it. His hand wanted to move, to wrap around their
throat and squeeze lightly, just to see their reaction. He could
hear their heartbeat, see the furious thump of it as a pulse
fluttered madly at the base of their throat, and was filled with
the strange urge to kiss it.

He looked back into those warm, gorgeous dark brown
eyes until it looked like they were going to burst into tears.
The scent of their arousal faded away quickly, replaced with
the stench of fear and apprehension.

Malachi recoiled, dropping his hand, feeling like he'd
been doused with a bucket of water. He turned away from
them—held his breath when he realised he was breathing a

bit too quickly.

"No." He took a deep, controlled breath.

"N-No?" Their voice sounded thick. He didn't know if they were disappointed or relieved. Oddly, it smelled like it was both.

"No." He remained turned away, wings flaring slightly and tail swishing, waiting until he heard the quiet shuffle of them putting their robe back on, before he turned around once more.

"I'm not sacrificing an animal," they said, their throat bobbing, their arms hugged almost defensively over their chest. "And I'm not selling my soul."

"Then what am I doing here?" Malachi snarled, eyes narrowed. He braced himself, preparing to disappear and wait until another human's call reached him through the Veil.

But how long could he wait? How long did Desmond have?

"No, wait, please." For the first time, the human looked truly desperate. "Is there anything else I can give you? Anything. *Please.*"

Malachi hesitated. It was those damning eyes. So pretty, with their long lashes. Or maybe it was their lips, so plump and pale. He wondered if they'd feel as soft and plush as they looked.

Or maybe it was the fact that Malachi was just as desperate for this contract as the human seemed to be.

Malachi should leave. He should say no. This attraction felt ... dangerous. Never in the eighteen months he'd spent in the mortal realm had he felt an attraction this visceral. He needed to cut his losses and leave now, find someone else. He had nothing to lose.

But as he stared into those pretty eyes, for some reason, it felt like he could see some of his own aching loneliness mirrored right back at him.

"Well?" Joy's voice came out unintentionally demanding. She swallowed, trying to reign in her desperation as she forced herself to meet the demon's red eyes. "There has to be something I can give you."

She was still trying to reconcile with the fact that she found a freaking *demon* almost painfully attractive. Then again, they were tall, dark, and handsome, and something about those fucking horns and those magnificent wings and that forked fucking tongue were *really* doing it for her, who'd have thought.

But when they'd looked into her eyes like they'd done earlier, like they'd been searching for something—Joy had forgotten, for a brief moment, where she was. It had been the position, she realised now; though they'd only used their knuckle, and their touch had been gentle, coaxing, it had taken her back to that night, to *him* gripping her jaw tightly in his grip, his fingers biting into her flesh and digging painfully into her bones, forcing her to look at him as he took what she'd never willingly gave.

"Your blood will suffice," the demon finally said.

Joy blinked. "My blood?"

"Yes." They licked their lips.

Joy trembled. "That's it?"

They raised an eyebrow. "Yes."

Joy's eyes narrowed. "I'd like it added to the contract, then. You can't trick or coerce me out of my soul."

The demon actually fucking rolled their eyes. "I can't take your soul if you don't consent, human."

"But you can *make* me *think* I consent, can't you? Under duress."

Their lips twitched. Their eyes seemed darker. "Yes," they admitted. "Fine. I accept. I swear I will not trick or coerce you into giving me your soul."

Demons were usually bound by their swears, Aunty Paloma had said. Joy glanced down at the knife she'd discarded, resting on the outer edge of her circle.

"How much blood are we talking?" The tip of her index finger still stung, though the bleeding had stopped.

"Nothing that will affect you seriously. A drop, perhaps." Those red eyes gleamed hungrily in her periphery.

Joy trembled again. Were demons nice? Considerate? Could they be? Last week, at Aunty Paloma's, for one moment, Joy had been sure she'd seen a glimpse of a dark-skinned, horned creature exactly like the one in front of her standing behind her aunt's sofa, it's clawed hands resting on Aunty Paloma's shoulders. But when she'd blinked, the apparition was gone like it'd never been.

She should've asked her aunt about it. Did Aunty Paloma have a contract with a demon? Why had it been touching her like that? Like a partner or—or a *lover.*

"Well?" the demon said, echoing her tone.

Joy glared at them. Their brow arched, their lips twitching.

Joy's lower belly did a weird somersault. She bent over, grabbing the discarded knife. She swallowed hard.

"How do you—?"

"Drop the knife." They eyed it with disgust, like it was a primitive instrument. It probably was, in their eyes. "Give me your hand." They were staring at Joy's left hand, at the finger she'd cut.

Fuck. Could they sense the cut? Or smell the source of her spilled blood?

Joy reached out, then hesitated when her eyes landed on the demon's sharp-tipped nails. She swallowed nervously.

"They won't hurt." Their lips twitched again. "Much."

Joy's stomach swooped. Were they fucking *flirting*? What the fuck.

The demon didn't slice her hand. No, they reached for her still-throbbing finger, pulled it into the hot, wet cavern of their mouth, and *sucked*.

Joy couldn't quite suppress the embarrassing sound that tumbled out of her, her body instinctively leaning forward, arousal pooling hot in her lower belly like lava.

It might've been a trick of her mind, but the red of the demon's eyes seemed to glow brighter. Their long lashes fluttered and they *groaned*, the sound raw with ecstasy.

Their tongue—which was smooth, firm and ridiculously slick—stroked against the cut on her finger, before wrapping around the digit like a fucking tentacle. It had her imagining for a wild moment how it'd feel between her legs, against her clit—*inside* her cunt. When the demon finally pulled her finger out of their mouth with a lewd sounding slurp, it was bleeding again.

The demon made a low, rumbling sound as they swiped at the cut with their forked tongue, like they didn't want to waste even a single drop, their eyes flashing. Joy's heart skipped a beat when those burning red eyes locked with hers. She swore she could feel the wound on her finger slowly closing up.

The demon stared at her magically healed finger with a hunger Joy couldn't describe, before they regretfully let it go.

Joy snatched her hand back, pressing it to her chest. Her pussy was slick and swollen, her clit *throbbing*, her heart slamming like a jackhammer against her ribs.

"Okay," she said, her voice high.

"Say the vow," the demon commanded, their voice rough.

Joy clenched her thighs together, locking her trembling knees to keep herself from dropping to the floor.

Her voice was still breathless when she recited, "Igris, entis, untis, represe."

The bond settled on her, like a golden thread behind her ribs, linked to the demon in front of her. When she touched her chest, instinctively reaching for it, she felt it pulse in answer, and knew it was the demon that had responded.

She dropped her hand, her cheeks burning, the evidence hidden underneath her melanin.

"The deal has been struck," the demon said. Their eyes glowed white as they spoke, and their voice now held a certain boom. It shouldn't have made Joy even wetter. "I will help you get the vengeance you seek."

TWO

"That's it? It's done?"

"It is done."

"Delicious," Joy couldn't help but say, even though she knew it made her sound like a cartoon villain.

The demon stepped out of the summoning circle. Joy instinctively took a step backward, her heart hammering. How did they seem even bigger now? Had their horns been brushing the ceiling before? And holy fuck, their *tail*. It was smooth, thick where it protruded from his lower back, and tapered to the end, with an upside-down heart forming its tip. As the demon moved, their smoky, shadowy robes rustled, their wings flexing and stretching wide. Fuck, those wings. Her eyes instinctively darted downward to the darkened area between their legs, before she quickly tore her gaze away with a flush.

She squared her shoulders and glanced at the clock. Icy

World would be closing soon; they needed to move now.

"What are you called, human?"

"You may call me Joy," she said, heading to her wardrobe.

She lived in what Nigerians referred to as a "self-contained", which consisted literally of only two rooms; the bathroom, and an area that served as the living room, kitchen, and bedroom, the former two split from the latter with a flimsy white net held up to the ceiling with thin black ropes nailed to the walls. Said nets were parted and pinned to the walls at the moment, looking out into the rest of the unit, but it did nothing to make the space feel more open.

The demon's presence should've felt invading in her small space, but it felt the literal opposite. Like they were meant to be here. Which was fucking ridiculous.

As she opened her wardrobe, she couldn't help but glance at her bed. She couldn't remember when last she'd had a proper sleep—at least, anything longer than an hour or two. But, what if—if she asked the demon to watch over her—

For a moment, desperate longing burned. Her eyes grew heavy with an almost painful exhaustion. It would feel so good—she would feel so refreshed—

She tore her gaze away from the neatly made mattress, furious. *Weak. Snivelling.* Did she really need a guard dog now, just to go to sleep? Fucking pathetic. *Grow a fucking spine, Joy.*

The demon tsked behind her.

She glanced at them, glaring. "What?"

Their lips twitched. "Humans give away their names so freely, so easily. I have never understood it."

"It's literally just common courtesy. It's considered polite."

"I acknowledge your explanation, but I refuse to understand it." Joy rolled her eyes. She bit the inside of her cheek when she realised she'd been about to smile, like the demon was her fucking *friend* or something. "What are your pronouns?"

"She/her. And you?"

"He/him."

"And your name?"

"You may call me Malachi. It is not my True Name, but it will suffice."

True Name. Aunty Paloma had mentioned something about it, about the power it held and how it was a double-edged sword; saying their True Name could give a demon untold power, but a human could also use it to bind them forever. The thought of using his True Name to keep him trapped and forced to do her bidding, whether he liked it or not, made her shiver with revulsion. She didn't want a slave.

"That's a nice name." The compliment was out before she could stop it.

Malachi's expression didn't change, but his wings fluttered, betraying his pleasure. Joy's stomach swooped.

"Thank you," he replied. "I thought so, too. That is why I picked it."

He sounded so proud of himself. Joy turned away quickly, finding herself blushing for some weird ass reason. She hadn't expected the demon to be so—so *human*. She'd been expecting, she didn't know—a sentient being that had no emotions at all. What even the fuck was going on right now. She resisted the urge to violently slap herself in the face.

"How do your powers work?" she asked, flipping through her wardrobe and taking out a black garment cover. "If I rip someone apart, bit by bit, can you put them back together and make it look like they'd died in their sleep instead?"

There was a pause. The demon's voice sounded darker, rougher when he responded, "Yes."

Joy refused to look at him. It should have disgusted her—

if a fucking demon was getting *aroused* at the thought of her vengeance, it should have filled her with pure, moral uprightness—it should have made her realise what she was doing wasn't fucking normal by any stretch of the imagination.

Instead, it made her lower belly swoop tellingly, making her clench her eyes shut. She was fucked up. *He'd* fucked her up, irreparably, and this was the proof. Not only did she want to relish seeing the life leave his eyes, but the fact that a freaking *demon* obviously approved of her plan had her almost swelling with pride. She was so fucking fucked up.

She unzipped the garment bag, revealing a blood red Ankara top and skirt decorated with small, white patterns in the shape of unfurling flowers. The flowers were unadorned—no lines or leaves—which made it seem like the starched, plain white material had been dipped in blood, but had missed a few spots. There was a slit on the right side of the skirt that went all the way up to mid-thigh.

Excitement made her pulse flutter. The knife in her sacrificial circle gleamed in the corner of her eye, but no, she was using an actual dagger for the occasion. It had been her father's, one of the few things he'd possessed that she'd managed to snag before his family had come swooping in like a kettle of vultures. She'd thought of using a gun, but it would have been downright impossible to acquire one in this country, and besides, she didn't want this to be over too quickly.

No, she wanted him to suffer, long and hard and slow. She wanted to watch the blood pour out of him until the life did, too, leaving his eyes blank and dull.

But one thing at a time.

She turned around. The demon—Malachi—was standing where she'd left him, outside the summoning rune, closer to the window. He was staring at her, like he didn't want to take his eyes off her for another single moment.

God, why was his gaze so—so *penetrating*?

She resisted the urge to cross her arms over her chest, even though her nipples were tingling. Her inner thighs still felt embarrassingly slick from earlier. Perhaps the "incident" had rewired her brain more awfully than she thought, because what even the fuck was happening.

"How long does the contract last?" She cleared her throat when her voice came out slightly breathless. She couldn't have him disappearing on her when she had so much planned to enact her revenge to her satisfaction.

"It lasts until we fulfil all the terms agreed," he replied.

So, until she killed *him*.

"Delicious." She grinned, knowing it looked slightly feral. "Do you have to leave? Do you sleep?"

His lips twitched. "I don't need it, but I can sleep if it is required. And I can leave if you wish it."

"Where would you go?" she asked curiously.

This time, it was his eyebrow that twitched. "My house?"

Joy blushed. "Demons have *houses*?"

"Yes. What did you think?"

"I don't know." Joy shrugged, still blushing. She turned away, reaching into her wardrobe for her makeup bag to hide the fact that she was hiding her hot face. Why did nothing about this, yet at the same time *everything* about this, feel so fucking normal? "I thought you just ... disappeared. Or went back to hell or whatever. I don't know."

""Disappearing" takes up a lot of magic. Contracts provide us with it, but not nearly enough for us to stay in the aether for that long. And while hell does have "houses", not all demons reside in hell."

That last sentence made her shiver; wasn't *that* the fucking truth.

"Wait, aether? Like in the horrible *Thor* movie?"

There was a brief pause. "I do not think it was that bad."

"Please," Joy scoffed before her brain was done processing. She spun around, gaping like a fish. "Wait, *you've* watched *Thor*? No, please don't answer that," she added quickly, spinning back around to face her wardrobe, her mouth still gaping. What the fuck, what the fuck, what the fuck.

The demon continued talking like nothing was amiss. "To answer your question, yes, the aether is indeed similar to what was referred to in the ... "horrible" *Thor* movie." She could fucking hear the air-quotes. "It is the thing that is all around us like air. The fifth element, as some humans call it. The ability to manipulate the aether is what your more supernaturally inclined humans call "magic"."

She shook off the absurdity of the rest of the conversation, and the fact that he'd watched fucking *Thor*, and not just *Thor*, but *Thor 3*. That seemed like a very important distinction. It implied he'd watched *1* and *2*.

Why was a demon watching Marvel movies?

"Right," Joy said, shaking her head. So, while she unfolded her plan, she didn't have to worry about him hovering over her shoulder all day and night. Though that would be kind of nice, if only—

No. *Down, Joy.*

"Great. Fantastic. Here's the plan."

So, the human was a she, and her name was Joy. Malachi found himself falling a little bit in love with her just because of her name alone, even though it was a contradiction to the woman before him. There was no joy to be found here. A riot of emotion poured from her frame, the most prominent of which was her hatred, and the focus on her plot for revenge. Malachi didn't think he'd ever tasted anything more fucking delicious. Except maybe her blood.

His ever-perpetual hunger clawed at his stomach, and he licked his lips, trying to chase the memory of the taste. Drinking human blood was frowned upon, even strictly forbidden in most sects; Malachi had never seen the effects himself, but there were several warnings of how ... addictive it could be. Based on the descriptions he'd heard, it was similar to a human imbibing alcohol or ingesting drugs. But based on the little of Joy's blood he'd tasted, that description could not compare. It had felt like taking a shot of pure euphoria; it had felt like being in the arms of his Sovereign, cradled and protected from all the hurts in the universe.

Joy was standing in front of a mirror now, wearing the dress that was splattered with red like blood. The dress was cut in half; the top didn't cover her shoulders, leaving them and the faint outline of her collarbones exposed. The skirt swept the floor, with a slit on the right side that went all the way up to her thigh. Malachi stared at the strip of brown skin in the middle of top and skirt, then at her exposed leg and thigh, thinking of how easy it would be to rip those flimsy straps off and tug the top down—or how easy it would be to grip the sides of the slit on her skirt, and rip until it came off completely, revealing every dip and curve of her naked frame beneath.

Malachi had witnessed unsuspecting humans in the throes of passion before, and even knew demons explored the same pleasures from time to time, but he'd never once felt the urge to partake in his baser desires. He nearly laughed. When would he have had the time? While he'd been held prisoner, back in his sect? Or while he'd spent the months after his escape hiding in the mortal realm, living like a hermit?

But right now, it felt like a cumulation of all the years he'd spent suppressing his emotions had come bursting to the fore. One look in her eyes—one inhale of her scent and one single taste of her blood—and Malachi had been rendered as animal as someone like him could be. Only all those decades-worth of rigid self-control kept him from begging her to let him feel what it would be like to sink into her soft flesh.

She'd merely combed her hair, a one-inch-high dark brown afro, her feet in killer strappy red heels that lifted her a few inches off the ground. Her mouth and nails were painted just as red as the dress, the colour doing absolute wonders for her warm brown skin.

With your help, I'm going to stalk him, she'd explained. *I'm going to follow him around like an apparition in his periphery, day after day, night after night, and just when he thinks he's about to lose his mind, only then will I go in for the kill.*

The matter-of-fact way she'd spoken of her revenge had made Malachi's lust worsen, had had him stiffening underneath his robes, his mouth flooding with saliva. God, her viciousness tasted so fucking *exquisite*. Desmond's greed for money and power always left a slimy aftertaste in the back of Malachi's throat, but something about Joy's bloodthirst burst in his mouth like sweet, fresh fruit.

Joy turned to face him, finally done with her face. He felt almost bowled over by her beauty. An ombre of black-to-red eyeshadow shaped her eyelids, making the brown of her iris and her skin seem almost luminous. Her brown cheeks were rosy, her red lips slightly shimmery with gloss. Once again, he thought of kissing her, of staining his mouth with all that red.

"I've always been a huge fan of the whole femme fatale persona, hence the getup." She gestured at herself, cocking her hip. "What do you think?"

"You look ... edible," Malachi said, his voice hoarse.

She blushed, the scent and sight of it making him feel weak in the knees.

Dangerous, his subconscious whispered. Demons had gone mad for less.

"Right." She cleared her throat. "Right," she repeated, her voice now clear, hard, as she refocused on her task. "How does this work? Do I have to drive? Or take a Bolt, rather; I don't drive."

Malachi felt the desperate urge to impress her. "Do you know where your victim lives?"

"No. But I know where he works," she said darkly.

"That's good enough." He reached out, his hand hovering in the air. "May I?"

For some reason, she became flustered. "Right, yes, okay," she said, reaching out to curl her fingers into the dip of his elbow.

Malachi sucked in a sharp breath at the feel of her touch. She seemed to be breathing quickly, too.

"Think of his place of work," he said gruffly.

He felt her instinct through the bond afforded to them by the contract, the pathways to said work, and reached out for the aether. When he took a step, she automatically did, too. Another, and they were standing across the road from a small supermarket.

"Holy shit," she said breathlessly. Malachi's chest puffed up without his control, his wings flaring behind them. "Are we—can people see us?"

"As long as I don't want them to, no. And no one can see me but you."

At least, not unless he let them. And even then, usually, he only let them see the more "human" version of himself, hiding his skin's unnatural colour, along with his wings, tail, and horns from their delicate sensibilities.

"Delicious." Her grip in his elbow tightened. His stomach did something funny at the action.

It was dark out, with few humans about. Malachi saw the opening times for the supermarket; it would soon close.

They waited. Joy's giddiness made Malachi feel a little drunk. She didn't seem to know demons could also feed on human emotion; everything she gave off, instead of making him feel full, had him nearly frantic for more. Taking the little bit of her blood as he'd done earlier had only made his hunger worse.

Malachi knew what it was to be hungry; he'd been hungry practically all his life. What was it about her that had his perpetual hunger going from easily ignored to downright unbearable? Almighty, he wanted to feast on her, in every way imaginable.

"There he is."

The man came around from the back of the store. He was on his phone. Still, Joy waited. Eagerness nearly had Malachi trembling. Wouldn't it be better to confront him in the darkness? Slit his throat when he slid into the driver's seat of his car?

Each scenario had Malachi's blood rushing with lustful excitement. Maybe it was the bloodlust seeping into him from the woman standing beside him, but Malachi absolutely wanted to destroy the man in the parking lot.

The man revved the engine, headlights coming on, flooding the street and across it to the pavement where he and Joy stood. As he eased out of the lot, Joy let go of Malachi's hand. Malachi felt her intention through the bond.

Tires screeched as the man slammed his foot on the brakes, staring at Joy's sudden appearance with wide, shocked eyes. She stood, back straight and eyes blazing in her blood-splattered Ankara dress, with a beautiful dagger clutched in her right hand, the blade glinting in the car's headlights.

When Malachi felt her intention through the bond, he manipulated the aether as easily as plucking the strings of a guitar, and rendered her invisible once more.

The man remained frozen in the lot for a moment, staring at where Joy had stood. Eventually, he shook his head and slid out of the lot.

He turned right, heading down the street. Malachi strummed at the aether when he felt Joy's intention once more, at the same time that the man glanced back through his rear-view mirror. His eyes widened again—Malachi strained to hear the way his heartbeat skipped, inhaling greedily as his scent went thick with fear—before he used his magic to hide Joy once again.

The man stepped on the accelerator, turning again on the next corner, disappearing into the night.

"Day one," Joy breathed, her grin untamed, her scent filled with satisfaction.

Malachi really, really wanted to get on his knees. He wanted to take her back to her bedroom, lay her down on her bed, and feast on her cunt until she came—again and again until she couldn't come anymore.

THREE

The success of last night hadn't yet left Joy's system. She was downright jittery as she watched the clock, counting down the hours until tonight when she could continue with her slowly unfolding revenge. A part of her just wanted to say fuck it and finish him off now, but she knew the reward would be so much sweeter if she took her time.

At closing time, Joy's boss, a.k.a. the manager of this branch of Shopwell, Mrs. Edochie, came up to her till, her heels clacking on the tiled floors. She was a tall, big woman—almost as big as Joy herself—and Joy had had more than one fantasy of being crushed between her thick thighs.

"Mrs. Edochie," she greeted politely. "Good evening."

"Ehen, well done. Just came over to ask if everything is going well? You managing the till okay?"

"Yes, thank you." She smiled. "Everything's all right."

"Wonderful. I'll bid you goodnight, then. See you on

your next shift. Don't forget to clock out."

"I won't." Joy echoed the goodnight.

She ignored the rest of her co-workers as she made it to the back to change, slipping earphones in her ears to prevent the small talk. She felt a pang as she watched them joke and laugh together, and forced herself to look away.

Acid burned in her stomach when she thought of her life before the incident. Her parents had died in a plane crash, and because the hatred was mutual on her father's side of the family, they'd split all his assets between them, leaving her with nothing. She'd tried to get a lawyer involved, but she'd forgotten this was Nigeria; the law only worked if you were rich, and respectability politics thrived in the veins of this nation: *you're only twenty-six and you have a steady job; the rest of the family is struggling, surely you understand, na*? She'd had to sell her mother's gold jewellery to afford her funeral and keep herself afloat for the few months following, cause God knows her father's side of the family wouldn't be paying for either.

Afterward, she'd gotten two jobs so she could pay her rent, keep food on the table, and aggressively market her graphic design business. By the time she finally landed a steady enough clientele that boosted her enough that she could quit both day jobs if she wanted, she'd looked up from the "grinding" table and two years of her life had gone by.

She'd decided then, something had to change. She would make new friends. Find a hobby. Get a fucking life. Maybe try dating again; she was twenty-eight years old and hadn't been with a single soul since she was twenty-three, having only her toys for company while she'd dealt with her grief and struggled to make ends meet.

So, when her former co-workers had invited her to the bar, she'd said yes.

She should have said no.

Joy slammed her locker shut. She was still new here, and her new co-workers weren't entirely comfortable with her just yet, so they didn't disturb her as she exited the mega mart.

Joy's plans since the incident were the same, except now it included her revenge. But every time she tried to imagine opening up to her new co-workers, something in her shrivelled up and recoiled, reminding her of the last time she'd done that. Which made her furious all over again, because she only felt that way because of *him*.

The supermarket might've finally closed, but the rest of the mall was still very much alive. She straightened her back, ignoring the creepy sensation that crawled along her spine every time she was in public. It always felt like there were eyes on her, now; it had felt that way since that night. Like everywhere she went, people were *staring*—like they knew, and they pitied her for it. Joy clenched her jaw, her hand gripping tight to the strap of her handbag, where, within, her dagger lay hidden in wait, wrapped in folded cloth. She didn't plan on doing anything with it, but it made her feel safer to have it on her person.

Joy hurried her steps. Sometimes, despite her need for revenge, she feared that she'd bump into him in a place like this, and he'd come to taunt her. Or worse, he'd try to converse with her like nothing happened, and even if she screamed and shouted and showed her discomfort, hardly anyone would intervene.

They were ridiculous scenarios, of course, because after the incident, when she'd thought going back to work and acting like nothing happened would make her look stronger— that it would make her look *better* than him—he'd pretended, too, laughing and cracking jokes with her and their co-workers as usual. She'd soon realised, with a bitter, soul-crushing epiphany, that his world had pretty much remained the same, while hers had been completely shoved off its axis.

It was far more realistic that if she accidentally bumped into him right now, she'd start viciously stabbing him and screaming her fury to the heavens. It was a tempting thought, but her plan to haunt him till she killed him would bring so much more satisfaction.

She turned on the next corridor, finally spying the exit. At the same time, someone left the shop to her right, nearly walking right into her.

"Oh, I'm sorry," the person began, then froze, their mouth audibly clicking shut.

The person was tall and slim, with warm, light brown skin. They were dressed in jeans and a t-shirt, their shoulder-length afro pulled up into a tight bun. In their left hand, they held a shopping bag, probably from the store they'd just exited, their purse in the other. The diamonds on their engagement ring glittered in the mall's bright lights.

Joy's first instinct was to ask what was wrong. Iyore only ever went shopping—outside of birthdays, holidays and other special occasions—when she was feeling stressed or upset.

"Joy," Iyore breathed. Joy didn't know if Iyore was surprised to see her, or scared.

It was probably the latter. Joy stared at her former best friend with what felt like horror. Memories of the last time they'd spoken flooded her, filling her with fury—with betrayal and anguish.

She began to shove past.

"Joy, wait, please," Iyore said.

Joy ignored her, stomping away faster.

She grabbed Joy's hand, tugging her back. Joy yanked her hand away and spun around, spitting, "Don't fucking *touch* me."

"I wanted to apologise!" Iyore cried.

"It's too little, too late."

"No, wait, Joy, you don't understand—"

"And I don't fucking care." Your best friend was supposed to believe you immediately when you told them you'd been raped. Your best friend wasn't supposed to ask what *you'd* done. They weren't supposed to ask if you were *sure*.

"Joy!"

Shame burned in Joy's throat as she remembered trying to *convince* her fucking best friend of the truth, and Iyore's response had been, "At least he's a fine guy; you should even be flattered."

And that had been the end of that. She hadn't planned on telling Iyore about her plan to enact vengeance, but it would have been nice to know there was someone in her corner, someone who acknowledged that what had happened to her had been awful and shitty, and should never have happened in the first place.

Her eyes burned. Fuck.

"Joy, please wait!"

Joy spun around again, her hand clenching into a fist. If Iyore didn't leave her alone, Joy was going to punch her in the throat.

"Me too!" Iyore yelled, forcing Joy to come to an abrupt halt. "Me too," she repeated, her voice barely a whisper.

Then she burst into tears.

They went to the seating area located by the lake. It was pretty at this time of night, the stars in the sky twinkling over the dark, unmoving surface.

Iyore hadn't stopped crying. Joy's heart was fucking breaking. They'd ordered drinks from the bar close by, just for something to do with their hands. Whenever people looked curiously in Iyore's sobbing direction, Joy glared at them with the force of a million suns, forcing them to quickly scurry away.

Iyore's sobs eventually died down. She took a huge gulp of her drink, then exhaled shakily.

"I-I wanted to apologise again," she began, her voice trembling. "You don't know how sorry I am, like, the minute I said those things—it was like I could *see* myself talking—it felt like something had come over me—but I know it's no excuse. I know I hurt you, all because I obviously haven't dealt as well with my own shit as I thought I had, and I just ..." She stopped, shrugging helplessly. "I'm sorry."

Joy took a deep breath, leaning back in her seat. "Well. This is supremely fucked up."

At least Iyore managed to crack a short laugh. "You're telling me."

"When did ..." Joy had to stop and swallow the sudden lump in her throat.

Iyore managed to pick up the silent question. She waved her hand limply. "Oh, it was a long time ago. We hadn't even met, by then."

Joy stared at her. Her limbs felt cold. "We met when we were eleven."

"Yeah." Iyore looked like she was going to cry again.

Joy felt filled with an indescribable rage. She wanted to ask who it was, but she didn't want Iyore living through her trauma again.

Like Iyore knew Joy wanted to ask, she filled in anyway. "It was m-my uncle. He'd been staying with us at the time." She quickly wiped her eyes. Her hands were shaking. "I remember telling my mum, and she ended up scolding me. Asking me why I'd been alone with him, then saying it's my fault because I was always s sitting on his lap because that was how he'd always tell me stories."

"Jesus fucking Christ."

"I mean, I did the same thing to you, so I can't exactly judge her."

"It doesn't matter. It's still really messed up."

Iyore nodded, her throat seemingly too thick to speak. They were silent again.

Joy's mind was racing. She couldn't imagine Iyore, a small, bright-eyed child of ten years old or less, being taken advantage of—being *violated* by her fucking uncle in her own fucking home. Then the gall of her own mother to—

Joy took a deep breath. Her voice didn't feel like her own when she asked, "Is he still alive?"

Iyore snorted. "Still invited to every family event."

Joy's hands clenched in her lap. She didn't know if she could contain the anger, the pure sense of injustice she felt.

"It's fine." Iyore shrugged jerkily. "I know not to go home when I know for certain he's going to be there. I haven't seen him face to face in years."

It didn't matter. It didn't fucking *matter*. Who else had he raped, over the years? Joy had been to Iyore's family gatherings; Iyore had five other siblings, and they were all married with little kids. What if he'd—

Joy's jaw ached with how hard she was grinding her teeth.

"It's been years, honestly. I forgive him, anyway. But that doesn't mean I can forget."

"Do you really forgive him?"

Iyore's hands formed fists against the wooden table. She didn't speak. It was answer enough.

Joy was going to kill him. The decision settled on her like a welcoming blanket. She was absolutely going to kill him.

She was going to fucking *destroy* him.

She glanced at Iyore, but knew she couldn't outright ask where the man lived. She thought of her demon. Could he find out where someone lived? But how would he, when he didn't have any information? Joy didn't even know the man's name, and she knew it would be really fucking odd to ask.

"Anyway, I noticed you deleted all of your social media," Iyore said, a falsely bright smile on her face. Joy let her change the subject. "And you changed your number. I h-hope it wasn't because of me?"

She'd asked the question lightly, like she didn't really care for the answer.

Joy couldn't help but soften. "It wasn't because of you."

"Oh." Iyore tried badly to hide her relief. She was never really good at hiding her emotions; always been an open book. "I guess you work somewhere in the mall, now?"

"Did you go looking for me?" Joy asked teasingly, though she was secretly pleased. She'd quit her job at Icy World a week after the incident. Even now, she couldn't believe she'd thought going back there—seeing his face every fucking day and acting like she wasn't bothered would mean she was *strong*.

She didn't want to be strong anymore. She wanted to be hurt. She wanted to be fucking *furious*.

"I did," Iyore said earnestly.

Joy's heart throbbed. She stood, coming around the wooden table, holding her arms open wide. Iyore eagerly fell into her embrace, holding her tightly.

"I know I don't deserve to ask for forgiveness," she whispered wetly into Joy's throat, "I know the things I said were all kinds of hurtful, so I know, despite whatever had made me act that way, you might still need time."

Joy pulled back from the hug to meet her eyes. They were

glistening. Joy's were, too. This was why Iyore was her best fucking friend—her soulmate, if soulmates existed. They'd tried dating in secret once upon a time, when things between them had gone heated in the privacy of their boarding house in Secondary School, but they'd never been brave enough to make it anything real.

Then they'd graduated, Joy had gone abroad to further her education, and back in Nigeria, Iyore had fallen in love with someone new. Through it all, they'd still remained close friends, and when Joy had returned back home with her Bachelor's and Master's in the bag, their friendship had picked up where it'd left off, like the years they'd spent apart had been nothing more than the blink of an eye.

"I do need time," Joy said, squeezing Iyore's hands in hers. "But thank you for talking to me. You didn't need to tell me any of that. It means a lot."

"I'm sorry. I'm really sorry."

"I know. I forgive you. I just need a little time."

"Yes. Of course. Anything you need."

"I love you."

Iyore's lower lip wobbled. "I love you, too."

Joy hugged her again. When she pulled back, she made a "gimme" motion with her hands. "Give me your phone. I'll give you my new number."

Iyore's eyes lit up, like Joy had given her the greatest gift in the world.

FOUR

While Joy was at work, Malachi used the opportunity to pay his other contractor a visit. He moved through the aether, and appeared in Desmond's little hut hidden in Mmuo, the forest that bordered the north of the city.

The little old man didn't even jolt when Malachi appeared out of thin air, though he did begin to cough violently. Desmond had a freaking mansion in the wealthiest estate in Arehjia, but this was where he'd chosen to come to die. Malachi wasn't necessarily surprised; without any true family or friends, of course the next best place the old man would want to take his eternal leave would be where the source of his power lay.

The hut held all his trinkets; little dolls made of straw, cowrie beads, animal bones and skulls, and a multitude of cloth stained in various, unappealing colours. Stacks of cash— both in Naira and Dollars—filled patterned bags in the corner of the small space, a physical representation of Desmond's ever-growing greed over the years. All that money, hoarded and wasted. He lay on a pile of mats in the middle, curled up on his side, his dark brown skin sweaty and ashen.

Their relationship had been strictly business from the start, but Malachi couldn't help but stare at him and feel ... something. Pity? Empathy? Desmond's contract had provided Malachi with an escape route from his sect, and he'd had the contract for nearly two years; it was expected he'd feel something for someone he'd been bonded with for so long.

"Useless," Desmond hissed when he was done coughing, his voice raspy.

And there went the empathy, gone like smoke.

The handkerchief Desmond had held to his mouth had a fresh splatter of red in the middle. Unlike Joy's blood, Desmond's blood did absolutely nothing for Malachi. Even his emotions were disgusting. Malachi had a theory after all his time spent on earth; each human and the emotions they gave off tasted differently depending on the human and their principles.

Desmond lied, stole, manipulated, and cheated, so everything about him tasted positively vile. Then again, Joy was literally plotting to slowly drive her victim mad before killing him, yet Malachi had never tasted anything more divine. Perhaps Malachi didn't understand after all.

"All that power," Desmond continued, "and you can't find a way to heal me?"

Malachi remained expressionless. Despite what Desmond thought, Malachi *had* tried to heal him, even though healing an ailment as extensive as this would take up way too much magic, and Malachi already had a limited amount of power as it was. But it seemed Desmond's shady dealings had come to a head; whatever was ailing him was magical in nature, done by someone—possibly another demon at the behest of a human—whose magic was more powerful than Malachi's. When Malachi had tried to remove the webs of magic, it had felt like chopping off the head of a hydra; where one fell off, three more grew in its place. He'd stopped for fear of making it worse.

He was sure Desmond had tried summoning another demon to help him, but other demons weren't willing or desperate enough to negotiate like Malachi; once they saw that Desmond's soul was already owned, they would simply leave him there without a word.

"Useless!" Desmond spat. He began to cough again, violently hacking away into his handkerchief. "Fuck, how long?" he asked. He sounded truly pitiful.

"Not long now," Malachi tried—and probably failed—to sound consoling.

Desmond had once demanded that since Malachi refused to heal him, then Malachi should end his suffering. Unfortunately, when Desmond had first made the contract, he'd made sure to add that Malachi could never, under any circumstances—be it physical or emotional—do anything to harm him.

Apart from that, demons weren't allowed to kill, not unless it was explicitly a part of a contract. The story Malachi had been told was that those who broke the rules were hunted down by what demons only referred to as "enigmas". The enigmas were supposedly the Almighty Sovereign's very own sentries, demons older than time itself, sent to make sure the precarious balance between the mortal and astral realm wasn't upended.

There were stories of demons who'd gotten greedy in the past, who wanted to take as many souls as possible in order to grow their power—only for the enigmas to find them, and rip them apart limb from limb.

They might have just been tales told to scare Malachi into being a good little soldier, but Malachi wasn't about to test its credibility.

"Will it—will it hurt?" Desmond coughed again.

And the empathy was back. "It will be like going to sleep," Malachi said gently.

Desmond sighed, closing his eyes. In a moment, he was fast asleep. By the time he opened his eyes again, Malachi would be gone.

Malachi reached for the thin thread that bound them; Desmond's contract, one out of two tethers now, keeping Malachi in the human world. It was so fragile he was almost afraid to tug at it, afraid that doing so would send it finally breaking apart.

Fear gripped him for a moment. What was Malachi going to do? Yes, he had his contract with Joy, but unlike Desmond's, it was only for a brief period of time.

What if owning Desmond's soul wasn't enough? Demons weren't meant to stay permanently in the human world, but could do so in one of two ways: using the bond formed from a contract as a tether, or owning a human's soul. Contracts ended; owning a soul was forever.

But the Priest—the sentries, even—had lived for thousands, if not *millions*, of years. Malachi hadn't even yet crossed his first tricennial, and had spent more than half of that starved and abused; surely owning one measly soul couldn't be enough?

He thought of long cold days and nights that bled into each other until time lost meaning. He thought of kneeling frozen on a stone slab, surrounded by four walls of concrete until the Priest needed him. He thought of the warmth and love flowing through the rest of the sect, their hymns reaching him down in the depths despite the thick walls, how it had nearly made him weep with anguish at the cruel torture of it.

He took a deep breath and shoved the rising panic and memories aside. If owning Desmond's soul wasn't enough, he'd figure out a plan later. He'll find a way. And if he didn't— if the sentries managed to find him first—

No.

Malachi would find a way. He *would* survive. After all, since leaving his prison behind, surviving was all he did.

Malachi thought of going back to his empty house located a bit deeper into the same forest, but the thought of it made him nearly physically ill. Almighty, he'd barely spent one day in Joy's company and already felt reluctant to be on his own again.

Fucking *dangerous.*

Joy seemed a little distracted when she finally came home from work that night. She didn't even react to his presence dwarfing her sofa, not like she had that morning.

After her body had forced her to take a twenty-minute nap before the sun had risen, she had nearly screamed his eardrums off when she'd sleepily left her bed and spotted his dark form sitting silently in her darkened living room.

"Jesus fucking Christ," she'd gasped after the ear-popping shout, clutching her chest, while Malachi had tried to keep the amusement off his face.

"Did you forget about me?" He couldn't quite keep the amusement from his voice, though, which had made her glare. "Honestly, Joy, I am hurt."

Saying her name had done something to her scent—made it go all bright and sweet. It was gone before he could properly taste what it was.

"I thought you had a house," she snarled.

He shrugged. "I need to stay close until the contract is fulfilled."

Joy's eyes narrowed, suspecting the lie for what it was, but she let it go.

"Don't touch anything while I'm gone," had been her last words before she'd left the flat, slamming the door and locking it behind her.

Malachi hated to admit it, but he'd felt an indescribable pleasure rise in him that, despite her reaction at finding him still here, she hadn't asked him to leave.

"Can demons eat food?" Joy asked distractedly as she made her way to the side of the room that held the kitchen. Her flat was a perfect square; from the front door, which was on the right corner of the south facing wall, was the sitting room; the kitchen was further in, on the left. The bedroom was directly behind the sitting room, with the bathroom opposite that, adjacent to the kitchen. "*Do* you eat?"

"We can, and we do."

"Noodles okay?" She got out four packs of Indomie. She glanced at him, her eyes trailing over his form, making his skin burn with it. She noticed his look and blushed, turning to add six more packs to the stack.

"Noodles are fine."

Joy's eyes narrowed.

"Can you really eat human food?" she demanded, hands on her hips.

His lips twitched. "Yes." He paused. "It provides no nutrients, but most of it tastes good."

"So, you don't *need* to eat it."

"I do not."

"Then I'm not wasting my precious Indomie on you."

He let out an airy chuckle. That bright, sweet scent burst

out of her again. Malachi had to clench his hands on his thighs to keep from leaning forward, to keep from snarling, *what the fuck is that?*

"Fair enough."

She returned eight packs to the cupboards, then brought a pot out, placing it under the sink, letting the water run.

"What *would* give you nourishment, then?" she asked, frowning curiously.

Malachi's voice was a low, husky timbre when he said, "I've come to realise that human blood does wonders for the body and mind." His eyes dropped to the finger on her left hand. A mixture of lust and hunger tore at his stomach, like nothing he'd ever felt before. Oh, Almighty. The Priests were right. He'd only taken a drop and he already felt addicted.

Joy seemed to be remembering the same thing. Her finger twitched, and he could smell the creamy sweetness of her arousal.

"A demon's true food, however, is emotion." His voice had never been this rough.

Joy couldn't help but spin around to face him again. "Emotion?" she asked incredulously.

"Yes."

"How does that even work?"

He stared at her for a moment, head tilted. "What do you know about demons?"

"Almost fucking nothing."

He let out another airy chuckle. Joy's lips twitched for a moment. And like clockwork, there was the sweet, bright scent. Was this the scent of her pleasure? Her happiness?

Fuck, Malachi had been wrong. If her bloodthirst tasted divine, then it was nothing on her happiness. He wanted to cause her to form that scent again—and again and again and again, just because.

"Demons are empaths, and I do mean that literally, not in

the way some humans seem to believe; we literally feed by absorbing emotion through our skin."

Joy's eyes trailed over his skin. "Really?" she said, a little breathlessly.

Malachi clenched his hands again. "It is supposed to make us more empathetic and understanding of each other, but ..." He shrugged.

His mind went back to his sect, to how they'd kept him away from the rest of the members, deliberately starving him until he was weak and easily manipulated. He remembered the Priest using his magic to embed a green gem into his chest, so when he sent Malachi to earth to mine for souls, all the emotions he might have fed on were redirected into the stone instead.

Malachi quickly shook the memories off. He was stronger now that he had two contracts, and would soon own Desmond's soul. He didn't have to worry about his sect coming for him for a little while longer.

He wasn't quick enough to hide his pain, because Joy was looking at him. *Really* looking at him—like she could see.

See *him*.

He stared back at her, making his gaze heavy and oppressive until she was forced to look away

Her throat bobbed with a swallow. "So, how did the whole deals with humans thing come about?" She frowned. "Wait, how did you even know blood could be "nourishing"?"

Malachi couldn't quite help his tiny smile. How was she so fucking cute? Like a little tiger.

"The deals have existed since time immemorial. Nicquiris like myself are tasked with bringing the souls and emotions of humans back to hell."

"What was that you just called yourself? Ni ...?"

"Nicquiri. It means "sensitive to the Veil". Humans able

to manipulate the aether or see through to "the other side" are also sensitive to the Veil, except, in the mortal realm, they are called witches or native doctors or magicians."

"So, only people—*demons*—like you, can go through the Veil?"

Malachi nodded. "It is what I was born to do." He tried not to sound too bitter.

"Oh." The expression on her face made Malachi feel strange. Her eyebrows were furrowed, like a frown, but her eyes—the purse of her lips—

Malachi sneered when he realised what it was. He didn't want her pity.

She looked like she wanted to ask more about his birth, but noticed his expression and swiftly changed the subject.

"And you take human souls for ...?"

"Human souls give demons unnameable power. There are demons who've fed on souls for thousands of years, equalling their might and power to that of a Sovereign's."

"Sovereign? You mean—a God?"

"Yes."

Joy looked like Malachi had just turned her entire world upside down

She shook her head quickly. "You know what? No. I'm going to make my Indomie, and I'm not going to think about any of this at all."

Malachi's lips twitched. So fucking cute.

He watched her move around the kitchen as she cooked. She put the noodles when the water was brought to boil, then began chopping vegetables. Onions, peppers, green beans, and carrots. It smelled really good. The whole thing took about six minutes to make.

She walked into the sitting room with her plate, hesitating at the sight of him. He was currently on the only piece of furniture meant for sitting in the entire flat.

She came to stand in front of him. When he still didn't move, she glared. He grinned, revealing his fangs.

Her breath caught, and he scented an exquisite mix of fear and arousal. *Interesting*.

"Move over," she commanded.

Malachi's dick stiffened. "Yes, ma'am."

He smelled her blush, though her expression didn't change. "Shut up."

There was nowhere for his wing to go unless he literally sat on it, so he left it where it was, slightly draped across the back of the sofa, the other one resting over the armrest and sweeping the floor on his right. She pretended not to see it as she sat, leaving barely two inches of space between them. His feathers brushed her back, and they both shivered. The space between them felt as infinite as it did finite, too much and not enough, making Malachi feel like he was going to vibrate out of his skin.

Resolutely ignoring his presence, she grabbed the remote of the ancient looking television from the floor at her feet, and turned it on.

"Cartoon Network, thank God," she muttered, and dug in.

The cartoon was about a blue cat and an orange fish. There was a hotdog and a robot and a floating eyeball—humans were so fucking mystifying. In all the time he'd spent on earth, with nothing left to do, he had consumed a lot of media; one thing he had never understood, much as he loved them, were some of the cartoons designed for children. Why were they so fucking random?

When the hotdog said "*delicious*", with a strangely familiar cadence, it took everything in him not to glance incredulously at the woman sitting beside him, even as his chest warmed with something he refused to name.

Seriously? *That's* where she got her catchphrase? Too

fucking cute.

She finished her food quickly, before the episode had finished airing. She practically skipped to the sink, the scent emanating from her making Malachi's mouth water.

"Day two," she said when she was done cleaning the dishes, that manic grin stretching her lips, bringing all of Malachi's senses alive. "I hope you're ready, demon boy."

His lips twitched. "Whenever you are, little tiger."

Her face did something complicated, like she didn't know if she liked the nickname or not. Her scent didn't lie, though. She liked it a lot.

Malachi had to stand, filled with restless, excited energy. Why had doing Desmond's bidding never felt like this? Was it because it had never felt so ... hands on? Desmond was a Native Doctor; folks mostly came to him for magical trinkets for good luck or bad luck alike, all of the items powered by Malachi's magic, since Desmond couldn't manipulate the aether himself. It was rare that Malachi ever got to do something truly dastardly.

Like last night, Joy took her clothes and changed in the bathroom. Malachi's breath hitched when she exited, even though it was the same outfit as before.

But it wasn't the outfit, was it? It was her aura; it was as though, when she put on the outfit, she put on a persona. What had she called it last night?

Femme fatale.

Joy sat at the bottom of her bed to put on her strappy heels, then went to the floor length mirror resting on the wall beside her front door to do her face.

She turned around when she was ready. Fuck, Malachi was beginning to become obsessed with wanting to get all that red on her lips stained on his own.

"Today, we're doing something different."

Joy couldn't count how many nights her rapist had stolen from her. Not only the night of the incident, but after, when she'd lost sleep, happiness—her sexuality and her own sense of safety. He'd made her feel like an interloper in her own skin, her own home.

So, Joy was going to return the favour.

He had another night shift. He usually did, back when Joy used to work here. That soul-crushing realisation came back; for him, nothing at all had changed. He kept the same job, the same hours, the same friends. He could fuck up the trajectory of her life irreparably, while still going on to live his. She wasn't even a blip on his radar.

Joy clenched the hilt of the dagger hard. Her jaw ached with how hard she was grinding her teeth.

Patience. Good things come to those who wait.

He finally exited the supermarket. It seemed he'd written off last night as a fluke, because he didn't even look across the street as he headed for his car. He got into the driver's seat, slipping his key into the ignition.

She spoke his name from where she and Malachi were seated.

His head whipped around quickly, his breath catching. Malachi was doing the work, keeping her invisible. The bond lent to them by their contract meant she didn't need to communicate what she needed from him. Which was extra fucking delicious.

Slowly, after a moment, her victim turned around and started the car. He looked up, into the rear-view mirror, right into Joy's bright eyes.

He sucked in a sharp breath, twisting around again, but

Joy was gone. Fuck, she wished she could hear his heartbeat right now. Was it pounding with fear and adrenaline, the way he'd made *her* heart pound? Was his breath catching in his throat—his lungs struggling to take in air?

She delighted in his heaving chest, his shaking hands as he once again reached for his keys. He hesitated, but didn't look in the rear-view mirror this time.

Joy's lips stretched wide, her blood rushing with ecstasy.

Malachi gently held her elbow. When she blinked, they were standing on the pavement.

Malachi waited until the car was about to turn down the corner, then he let go. At the same time, like *he* couldn't resist, he looked in his rear-view mirror.

Joy grinned again. She lifted the hand that held the dagger, and waved. He stared at her, eyes wide and stricken, as he turned and disappeared around the corner.

"Day two," Joy whispered.

"You said you feed on emotions," Joy began the moment they were back in her tiny little accommodation. She spun around to face Malachi, her eyes gleaming. Her excitement was infectious, making Malachi's own blood rush just as fast. "Did you taste his? Was he afraid?"

"Petrified," Malachi replied honestly, his voice husky.

"Good," Joy growled, pacing, like she couldn't keep still. "Oh, so fucking good. I can't wait to fuck him up. I can't wait to absolutely destroy him."

Malachi was prowling toward her before he realised what he was doing. She noticed, but she didn't look afraid. In fact, the scent of her intensified, her euphoria from the successful night of hunting her victim quickly compounding with the scent of something thick and almost eager.

She stumbled when he was finally upon her, like his aura alone was enough to knock her off-balance. His hand easily went around her waist, steadying her, pressing her against him. Feeling her warm softness pressed against him nearly had Malachi's brain igniting from the sensation. Her palms pressed flat to his chest like she wanted to shove him away, but she made no move to do so. She tilted her head back, meeting his eyes. Her throat bobbed with a swallow. The scent of her adrenaline was bleeding into something darker, something more sensual.

Malachi finally did what he'd been dying to do since they'd returned; he pressed his thumb to the centre of her lips. She inhaled shakily. He swiped the digit across the soft, pouting flesh, spreading the red of her lipstick until it stained her cheek and jaw like blood.

Fuck.

Her pupils had swallowed up her irises, her eyelids at half-mast. She was almost panting.

"Sweet, murderous Joy," Malachi husked, his wings flaring, wanting to wrap around them both, like he could shelter them from the world. "You are exquisite."

Her eyes dropped to his mouth, her lips parting. Her breaths were so fucking warm. "I—"

His tail flicked, wanting to join in on the fun. It found the slit of her dress and slid between her legs, tracing up the sensitive inside of her thighs.

It broke the spell. She jerked out of his arms, one hand grabbing the opening to her skirt, squeezing it closed. Her other hand went almost protectively around her breasts.

"Don't ..." She couldn't seem to know how to finish the sentence. "Just—don't."

Malachi didn't move as she practically ran. She pulled down the netting that hid her bed from the rest of the room, then just stood there. The netting was thick enough that he could only make out her silhouette, and nothing more. In the sudden hush, her breaths seemed very loud.

"Do you wish for me to leave?" he forced himself to ask.

He shouldn't have pushed too far. He shouldn't have done anything at all. He should have—

"Do what you want," she replied flippantly. He watched her form twist away from him, heading for her wardrobe.

Malachi's chest lit up. That wasn't a rebuke. With a barely-there smile, Malachi silently headed for the sofa and sat so his back was to her, giving her privacy.

For some reason, he knew, like last night, she probably wasn't going to sleep. He wondered if it was healthy—didn't human adults need at least six hours a night? But he'd already done enough to disrupt her today, he wasn't about to do more.

They sat in silence, and Malachi basked in how nice it was, even though they didn't speak, to be in the company of another after he'd spent so long on his own.

And when she was finally forced to sleep, when dawn was just threatening in the horizon, Malachi felt a sense of peace he'd strived to feel what felt like his entire life.

FIVE

Some part of Joy knew she was dreaming. Since the incident, she fought so hard not to sleep, but some nights, her exhaustion managed to catch up on her, forcing her eyes to close, plunging her into a sleep she did not want because in sleep was where her demons resided. Her *real* demons, that is, not demons like Malachi.

At one point, she'd thought if she was exhausted enough, she'd simply black out and wake up none the wiser. She'd soon realised that no matter how tired she was, she would always be plunged into a more sinister version of the same nightmare.

She was walking up the stairs to her former flat, happy about something, though she couldn't quite think of what. She was stumbling—she was drunk, which was weird, because she never drank so much as to lose her inhibitions, but the reason was explained away. She leaned against the

Joy trembled with satisfaction. She'd made him look like that, all without once touching him.

"Gotta head to work soon," she said, winking at him, pretending she didn't care one bit about her nakedness as she headed for the bathroom.

She'd thought the closed bathroom door between them would break the spell. Now the shame would come. Now the clarity would return, and she'd ask herself what the fuck she'd done. There was supposed to be disgust, self-hate—

But all there was was pleasure.

SIX

It had been hours since their little tryst, and Malachi still felt primed like a fucking bull. He could hardly take his eyes off her—had to keep his hands clenched in his lap like it would keep him from doing something reckless. He couldn't believe that was his first sexual experience with another being; it was no wonder some humans were obsessed with it, if that was how it felt.

Almighty, looking back, he didn't know how the fuck he'd managed to keep himself from touching her. Okay, that was a lie; he hadn't touched her because she hadn't wanted to be touched. He'd tasted enough in the delicious cocktail of emotions she'd been giving off to know the moment had been all about her, not that Malachi minded in the least. In fact, he'd felt downright honoured she'd let him witness her reclaiming her pleasure.

Joy acted like nothing had happened, like she hadn't

made Malachi come so hard—without even once *touching* him —he could still feel it in his dick hours afterward. She'd had an early shift today, which meant she was back before nightfall. They still had time before she continued with her torture.

When she was done making her meal—yam and egg sauce— she came over to the sofa.

Her scent went sweet and warm, nearly making Malachi sway forward like she was magnet and he was metal, his mouth flooding with saliva.

"Move," she commanded.

Malachi silently did as he was told, his throat too thick to speak. Like last time, he left his wing lying across the back of the sofa.

Unlike last time, when Joy sat, she let her back rest against the chair—against his wing. She was wearing nothing but a tank top and a flimsy little jean skirt that did absolutely everything for her round ass and thick thighs. His feathers brushed against the skin of her bare shoulders and back.

They both trembled.

Joy's breaths seemed a little fast. He saw her glance quickly at him from the corner of her eye.

"Can you feel that?" she asked, her voice a little husky. She rolled her shoulders for good measure.

"Yes," Malachi gritted.

"Right. Okay." Her voice was breathy. "Are you—I'm not hurting you, am I?"

"No." At least, not in the way she thought.

A different kind of hunger built up in Malachi's stomach— the desperate hunger to be touched, in any capacity. He didn't care if it was her fingers brushing against his, or her thigh pressed against his own; Malachi had never wanted to be touched this badly in his entire life.

"Okay, I don't know if I can keep doing this. I feel bad."

Malachi blinked at her. "I don't understand."

She waved at him with her free hand. "I can't just—it doesn't feel right. It doesn't matter if it does nothing for you; I should still make you a plate. It's only right."

Oh. She was ... she didn't like that he wasn't eating? That was—Malachi felt strange, suddenly. Like his skin was too big for his body.

"I'm fine."

"What did you say you ate again? Emotions? Are my—wait—" Her mind worked furiously. "Does that mean you know what I feel at any given time?"

"I can hazard a pretty good guess, yes."

"Oh my fucking God. You know what? No. I am not dealing with the implications of that right now. Are my emotions enough? Are you feeling properly ... nourished?"

A sweet ache burned in Malachi's chest. He rubbed it distractedly. He felt so exposed. Vulnerable. Which made no fucking sense.

"Joy," he said, waiting until she met his eyes. "Trust me when I say this: I have never in my life felt more full."

She stared at him, eyes wide, her scent going all soft and warm. Malachi wanted to bury his face in her throat and inhale for the rest of eternity.

She cleared her throat. "What about my blood?" she seemed to force herself to ask, her voice breathless. "If you—that is, would it be—?"

Malachi's eyes darkened. Saliva flooded his mouth. "I really am fine, I promise."

She stared at him. "Are you really sure?"

For a moment, Malachi couldn't speak. He was used to going hungry. After spending so much time isolated back in hell, when he'd finally broken the Priest's gem and escaped his control, all that emotion flooding him from the earth and the humans around him had been too much.

So, he'd isolated himself again, only using the sparse visits he made to Desmond to feed.

He was used to being hungry, *all* the fucking time. He hadn't lied when he'd told Joy he'd never felt this full. Last night had felt like the first full meal he'd had in his entire life; he could have gone at least a few more days before the hunger pangs returned.

But right now ...

"Great. Decision made," Joy said, seeming to take his silence as an answer.

She thrust out her hand.

"What are you ...?" His tongue felt too heavy for his mouth. He was sure his eyes were almost entirely black, hiding the red of his iris.

"Go on." Fuck, her *scent* right now. Lust and determination. She *wanted* him to drink her blood. He felt almost drunk with it. "Just ... don't take too much."

Malachi took her hand, though he tried not to look desperate. He wouldn't take too much; after the last time, when he'd first broken the Priest's control and tried to gorge himself, it had had him feeling sick for days afterward. He wouldn't make that mistake now. He would take a little, and this time, he would savour it.

His tongue unfurled, sliding out of his mouth.

He heard Joy's heart thump. "H-Holy shit." The scent of her arousal increased.

"Do you mind if I bite?" Malachi murmured, licking across the pad of her thumb, the slit at the forked end of his tongue parting around the digit.

"Jesus," she rasped, looking like she was trying not to squirm. "No, I don't mind. You can—"

Malachi sucked her thumb into his mouth, then gently pierced her flesh with one of his sharp teeth. Her scent went bright with pain, but was soon drowned out by the scent of pleasure.

Her blood ran down his throat, thick and hot and fucking delicious. Malachi moaned, sucking again. Vaguely, he could feel that he was hard, his dick straining between his legs. His tongue wrapped around her thumb, as if to keep her from pulling away.

She was panting and squirming now, staring with dark eyes at his mouth.

Another, Malachi told himself, as he sucked again. *Just one more.* His eyes rolled back, another groan escaping him as more of her blood poured into him. Fuck, it felt like her emotions affected the taste of her blood, too; the first pull had held the bitter tang of her pain from his bite; the second had been filled with a sudden rush of pleasure; and this pull was rich with the creamy sweetness of her arousal.

Malachi jerked her thumb out of his mouth with a lewd sound. He used the aether to seal the wound shut.

He wanted to come. Just shove his robes off and tug on his dick until he spilled all over himself like last night.

"Oh my God." Joy was trembling.

Malachi pressed a kiss gently against her knuckles, ignoring his desperate arousal.

"Thank you," he husked, letting her hand go.

"You're welcome," she whispered, placing her hand primly in her lap.

Their eyes met and held. Malachi, for some odd reason, suddenly found his lungs struggling to function. Her gaze fell to his mouth. His own fell to hers. Neither of them moved, the tension between them so sharp it could have sawed through titanium.

Joy abruptly shot to her feet. "I should get ready."

Malachi swallowed. "Right. Yes. Of course."

He scrubbed his hands over his face when she disappeared into the bathroom. He didn't touch himself, even though he could hear little, bitten-off moans—even though he could taste her pleasure and arousal in the air.

The combination of her taste in his mouth and her scent in the air was almost too much. His eyes rolled back, his hips lifting slightly off the seat when she finally came, the rich scent alone nearly enough to have him shooting untouched into his robes.

He'd calmed down somewhat when she finally exited the bathroom, dressed in her signature red and white.

Malachi stood.

Joy smelled like satisfaction, but unlike last night, her desire still lingered underneath. She still wanted—

Malachi forced the thought aside. That scent was not an invitation.

"Ready, demon boy?" Her lips twitched.

"Whenever you are, little tiger."

Joy's finger still tingled. Despite her quickie in the bathroom, she still felt on fire with it. God, she didn't think she'd ever wanted anyone this badly, not even when she'd wanted Iyore back in Secondary School—when sneaking around to fumble underneath each other's clothes here and there had felt like being struck with lightning, every single time. The only thing keeping her from jumping Malachi's bones right now was her still unfolding revenge.

This time, when her victim came out of the supermarket, he did so slowly, his eyes darting across the street. When he opened the door to his car, he glanced around the back seat first, before sliding into the driver's seat.

Joy wondered, if she'd still had her old number or her social media accounts active, if he would have tried to contact her after seeing her ghost everywhere. Would he try to threaten her? Or would he pretend he wasn't slowly losing his mind? The only part of her Before the Incident that she'd left up was her graphic design website. It was her main source of income, and she'd be damned if she shut that down because of him.

She'd merely sent an email to her regular clients and left a message up on her website that she had a family emergency and wouldn't be taking any new clients or commissions for some time.

She hadn't checked her email since then. She wondered if he'd sent her an email after she'd blocked his number—before she'd decided to change her number altogether; disappeared abruptly from work; and then again from the internet. The thought had her clenching her hand around her dagger.

Malachi, through this mystical bond they shared, sensed Joy's intention.

"May I?" he asked, his hand hovering over her hip.

Joy's heart leapt into her throat. She glanced at his wings, her eyes wide. Of course they couldn't just disappear through the aether; she didn't know where her victim lived, and flying would be the easiest way to follow him to find that out.

Malachi's wings twitched when she stared at them for too long. When she glanced at his face, he was smirking slightly. "My wings certainly aren't there for decoration."

Joy's cheeks went hot. "Shut up. And yes, you may."

His hand slid around her waist, pulling her close and pressing her firmly to his chest. His wings beat hard, lifting them off the ground. Joy bit back a squeak, throwing her arms around his torso for balance, hiding her face in his throat, too afraid to look down.

"I've got you." Malachi's voice rumbled in his chest, the

sound melting in her stomach, heating her up between her legs.

The wind rushed over her, the beat of Malachi's wings almost unbearably loud. Joy wanted to look around, enjoy the flight cause she'd probably never get to experience it again, but she was too afraid. She used the opportunity to shamelessly enjoy Malachi's embrace instead; he was literally holding her up with *one* single arm, holy shit. Every inch of him was hard and firm—practically *made* for snuggling. Or humping.

Down, Joy.

When they finally began to descend, Joy felt a pang of disappointment mixed with relief. She braved looking out from Malachi's chest, only to find that they were in one of the more affluent estates in Arehjia. Joy's lip curled. Of course he lived in a place like this. Probably on his parents' money, while he worked small jobs in supermarkets specifically to prey on vulnerable people like Joy.

They landed on the ground just as her victim exited his car.

His shoulders seemed to relax when he entered his house, locking the door behind him, Joy and Malachi slipping easily inside with Malachi's reality-bending magic.

Joy almost laughed. Oh, he felt safe here, did he? Well, that was about to fucking change.

She stalked past him, still rendered invisible by Malachi's power. When Joy found his sitting room, she stood in the middle and waited. Malachi trailed silently behind her victim, his robes and his wings making him look like a wraith—like the grim reaper himself.

Her victim came in, oblivious, pulling his phone out of his pocket at the same time that he reached for the light switch.

He literally screamed as the lights came on, and Joy

appeared in all her vengeful glory, her eyes bright, her dagger held aloft. She was there for only a blink—so fast he'd probably think he was hallucinating.

He stood, blinking repeatedly, staring at where she'd stood —where she was *still* standing, invisible to his eyes. His hands were shaking.

"Delicious," Joy said viciously. She didn't need to see any more. Malachi walked to her and took her elbow. They went through the aether, and appeared back in her living room.

Almost the moment they did, Malachi stumbled.

Joy instinctively grabbed his arm and his hip, keeping him from losing his footing.

"What the fuck," she gasped. "What was that? Are you okay?" Had doing the invisible thing taken more strength out of him, after all?

Malachi's face seemed twisted with something not quite painful. He regained his balance, straightening slowly. Joy reluctantly let go.

His eyes landed on hers, heavy with something she couldn't interpret. It made her heart pound with fear.

"I'm afraid I must leave for a bit, if that is okay with you."

Joy stared. What? Her first instinct was a rise of alarm. She wanted to immediately say fuck no, he couldn't just *leave*. What if she needed him?

On the heels of that was panic. She didn't need him. She didn't *need* anyone.

She turned away from him, shrugging jerkily as she stalked to the sink. "Do whatever you want. You don't need my permission."

Malachi didn't respond. Joy didn't dare look back. She washed her dagger, one of her many rituals after her hunting. When she turned around, Malachi was already gone.

Her stomach twisted and turned all over itself. She'd gotten this place specifically because she could see all four corners of it—specifically because of how small and cosy it was; how it had made her feel safe.

Now, in Malachi's sudden, unexpected absence, it felt almost cavernous. How had she gotten so used to his presence in such a short amount of time?

She felt almost ... naked, without him here, which only increased her panic. She couldn't be feeling like this— whatever *this* was. She needed to remember she only needed him so she could enact her revenge without consequences. She needed to take several steps back, ASA-fucking-P.

Her revenge would soon be coming to an end anyway, and then she wouldn't need Malachi anymore; she would never have to ever see him again.

Her chest constricted painfully. She blamed the sudden, panicked racing of her heartbeat and the empty hollowness in her stomach on her annoyance, and nothing else.

Malachi stared down at Desmond, still stubbornly clinging to the last wisps of his life, while Joy's last words rang through his skull.

Do whatever you want. You don't need my permission.

Her emotions had betrayed her though, her heartbeat stuttering at the lie. Malachi's heart had warmed at how fucking adorable she was, at the same time that her words had reminded him of what this was.

To Joy, no matter what her emotions said, Malachi was simply a means to an end. Her panic at him needing to leave for a moment had nothing to do with how she felt about him, but everything to do with what she needed him to do for her.

It was just the plain truth, but it still tore savagely at

Malachi like someone was shredding apart his skin and bones. Almighty, he'd had one single *taste* of companionship— of what it could simply *feel* like—and he'd folded like a— what was the end to the metaphor again? Right. A fucking *pretzel*.

Just what the fuck did he think he was doing here? Did he think, that just because she'd let him watch her come, that she'd let him take some of her blood, that she suddenly—

She suddenly *what*? Malachi didn't even know what he wanted her to want. What did *he* want?

What was he *doing*?

The thin bond in his chest snapped as Desmond finally took his last breath. For a moment, everything was still, then there was Desmond—or what the human's called his "soul". It rose from the bag of bones and flesh on the ground, a brilliant, stunning ball of light.

It flew through Malachi's body, and he gasped, stumbling, as he was filled with so much power and energy he couldn't describe it. The Veil fluttered in front of his eyes, Malachi's heart pounding erratically as he saw the place he'd been created for the first time in a fucking long time, then Desmond's soul was gone, through the Veil and off to continue on his journey in the afterlife.

Malachi savoured the power flooding his veins; he felt taller, stronger. He hadn't even noticed the subtle strain he'd been holding in his temples all this time—the strain of keeping himself tethered to a plane in which he didn't belong.

Until now—until he was flooded with *true* power.

The feeling was reminiscent of something in his past. Malachi reached for it, and was plunged into vivid memory.

The arms of his Sovereign, cradling him after he was born. There was another—a sibling?—pressed close to his side. The love from his creator—his nurturer—felt all

"You just ... get unnameable power from ... essentially owning them?"

"That is correct."

"So ..." She was beginning to squirm, and her scent went all hot and smoky, making Malachi's mouth abruptly start watering. "So, if, for example, I sold my soul to you, how would—?"

Malachi's mind went blank for several seconds. He swallowed repeatedly, but saliva kept flooding his mouth. Owning Joy's soul—

Need and possessiveness like he'd never felt before seized his limbs, and he had to clench his hands into fists again to keep from reaching out, to keep from touching her. If she hadn't been resting against his wings, they'd have flared wide to show his intention.

"If you sold your soul to me, then your soul would belong to me," he said simply, his voice rough.

"And it doesn't ... it doesn't *do* anything to me?"

"It does not."

"You can't—I won't, like, become your slave? Or die on the spot?"

His lips twitched. "No."

"Huh." She sounded thoughtful. "But I'll definitely go to hell, right?"

"Oh, yes. That is a given."

He'd thought that would make her finally come to her senses, but no, she still smelled ... interested.

Malachi dug his claws into his palms.

"So, the more contracts you make—or rather, the more humans sell their souls to you, the more power you have."

"That is correct."

Joy went silent again. The lights abruptly went out.

"Oh, for fuck's sake. Fucking NEPA."

Neither of them moved. Malachi had learned, after the

Malachi like someone was shredding apart his skin and bones. Almighty, he'd had one single *taste* of companionship— of what it could simply *feel* like—and he'd folded like a— what was the end to the metaphor again? Right. A fucking *pretzel*.

Just what the fuck did he think he was doing here? Did he think, that just because she'd let him watch her come, that she'd let him take some of her blood, that she suddenly—

She suddenly *what*? Malachi didn't even know what he wanted her to want. What did *he* want?

What was he *doing*?

The thin bond in his chest snapped as Desmond finally took his last breath. For a moment, everything was still, then there was Desmond—or what the human's called his "soul". It rose from the bag of bones and flesh on the ground, a brilliant, stunning ball of light.

It flew through Malachi's body, and he gasped, stumbling, as he was filled with so much power and energy he couldn't describe it. The Veil fluttered in front of his eyes, Malachi's heart pounding erratically as he saw the place he'd been created for the first time in a fucking long time, then Desmond's soul was gone, through the Veil and off to continue on his journey in the afterlife.

Malachi savoured the power flooding his veins; he felt taller, stronger. He hadn't even noticed the subtle strain he'd been holding in his temples all this time—the strain of keeping himself tethered to a plane in which he didn't belong.

Until now—until he was flooded with *true* power.

The feeling was reminiscent of something in his past. Malachi reached for it, and was plunged into vivid memory.

The arms of his Sovereign, cradling him after he was born. There was another—a sibling?—pressed close to his side. The love from his creator—his nurturer—felt all consuming, almost painful in its intensity. The feeling filled Malachi up until he found himself naturally returning it, only for it to pour back into him, a feedback loop of pure happiness.

It was shared between three of them, bouncing between them and amplifying until Malachi felt like *more* than just himself—larger than his existence, larger than the universe.

Then, just when he'd been introduced to the well of love and belonging that was the rest of the sect, the Priest and the sentries came. He was pulled from his Sovereign's arms, his sibling pulled in another direction. Guiling, trustful, still brimming with the joy of his existence, he'd followed, frowning only when he was within the four walls that would become his prison for what was meant to be the rest of his life.

Malachi let the memory stop there, going back instead to how it had felt to be loved, even if it had only been for just a moment.

He understood it first-hand now, why the sects were obsessed with collecting human souls. Apart from the power it brought, Malachi was sure he would never feel this strong sense of love and sheer completeness in his lifetime again.

Unless he took another. Malachi's hands clenched by his sides. He didn't dare think of Joy, of what it would feel like.

He needed to find another contract soon, just in case, probably before the one with Joy ended. After that, he would go back to his house in the woods until that new contract ended, and the cycle repeated itself again.

Once upon a time, that cycle had felt like safety. Now, though, it was beginning to feel like just another kind of prison.

SEVEN

Joy was sitting cross-legged on her bed when Malachi returned. She straightened imperceptibly at his appearance, and even though Malachi could tell she was trying to suppress her emotions, he could scent her immediate relief. Malachi immediately felt pleased, though he tried to pretend he wasn't.

Joy was seemingly watching the TV from all the way on her bed, pretending valiantly that she couldn't see him standing there. Malachi walked until he was standing in front of the sofa, raising an eyebrow when she still refused to look in his direction, her expression stubbornly expressionless.

Malachi turned around and sat. His heart felt swollen underneath his ribs. They were silent for a moment, the silence filled with tension, before Malachi spoke.

"I have been wondering," he said, not turning to look at

her, though he could now feel her gaze boring into the back of his head, "what did your victim do to you that requires such calculated revenge?"

At first, he didn't think she would reply. Then she took a deep breath.

"He raped me," she said matter-of-factly.

Malachi stiffened. His eyes were suddenly filled with red. He realised, faintly, that he was digging his claws into his palms.

"I see," he said, sounding light, even to his ears. "Then I am glad he will soon meet his end."

Joy snorted. Malachi's lips twitched without his permission. The scent of her happiness—a burst of something airy and bright—had him clenching his hands once more.

And so what? He suddenly thought, almost viciously. So what if Joy was using him? So what if he couldn't have her after this? So what if he never saw her again? Was he going to pretend he didn't want her *now*, just because their contract would soon come to an end?

"Are you really planning to watch the TV from all the way over there?" he asked, still not looking at her from over his shoulder.

There was a brief silence, then he heard her leaving the bed, shuffling over to the sofa. She didn't look at him as she growled at him to move over, and Malachi felt so fucking hot, everywhere.

On the TV was Joy's favourite cartoon, of the blue cat and the orange fish; her scent always grew so light and lovely whenever she watched it.

"What did you have to do, anyway?" she said, her eyes practically boring into the TV. She was picking at a thread at the bottom of her skirt, all signs screaming she didn't really care about the answer.

Her scent said otherwise. Almighty, Malachi wished he could move closer. He wanted to touch her, so fucking badly. Hold her hand maybe. Something. Anything.

"I had a contract before yours. The human just died."

Joy finally whirled around to face him. Malachi nearly trembled at finally having those doe eyes on him.

"Did you—did he—?"

His lips twitched with amusement, despite himself. "No, I didn't kill him."

Joy blushed.

"He died from natural causes. I just went back to take what I was owed."

It took a second for it to dawn. Joy stared at him with wide eyes. "His soul."

"Yes." Malachi wondered what she was thinking.

She looked away, her mouth working for a moment. "Did you—how do you—do you just eat it, then?"

"What?" Malachi replied, unusually inarticulate.

Joy glanced at him from the corner of her eye. "His soul. Do you just eat it?" She tried, but she couldn't quite hide her revulsion, and her fear.

Malachi nearly laughed, but he couldn't blame her for her ignorance.

"Demons are awarded power in two ways; by making a deal with a human, and by having a human sell their soul. Desmond's contract was that I be by his side until the end of his natural life, which meant I could not fully own his soul until our contract ended—that is, until he died. But the moment he did, his soul was mine. He has gone off to continue his journey in the afterlife, while I have taken the essence of him as he had been on earth."

"Oh." Joy still looked slightly confused. "So ... demons don't eat souls."

Malachi's lips twitched. "We do not."

"You just ... get unnameable power from ... essentially owning them?"

"That is correct."

"So ..." She was beginning to squirm, and her scent went all hot and smoky, making Malachi's mouth abruptly start watering. "So, if, for example, I sold my soul to you, how would—?"

Malachi's mind went blank for several seconds. He swallowed repeatedly, but saliva kept flooding his mouth. Owning Joy's soul—

Need and possessiveness like he'd never felt before seized his limbs, and he had to clench his hands into fists again to keep from reaching out, to keep from touching her. If she hadn't been resting against his wings, they'd have flared wide to show his intention.

"If you sold your soul to me, then your soul would belong to me," he said simply, his voice rough.

"And it doesn't ... it doesn't *do* anything to me?"

"It does not."

"You can't—I won't, like, become your slave? Or die on the spot?"

His lips twitched. "No."

"Huh." She sounded thoughtful. "But I'll definitely go to hell, right?"

"Oh, yes. That is a given."

He'd thought that would make her finally come to her senses, but no, she still smelled ... interested.

Malachi dug his claws into his palms.

"So, the more contracts you make—or rather, the more humans sell their souls to you, the more power you have."

"That is correct."

Joy went silent again. The lights abruptly went out.

"Oh, for fuck's sake. Fucking NEPA."

Neither of them moved. Malachi had learned, after the

first few times and after he'd read up on it, that the power constantly—and unpredictably—going in and out was a normality in Nigeria, which was kind of bleak. And annoying.

He stilled when he scented—

"Are you okay?" he asked sharply.

Joy was breathing hard. "I'm—I'm fine."

Malachi gave her a moment to herself. He wanted desperately to move closer, to offer her comfort, but the thought of asking to do so made him feel too vulnerable.

"Ever since—" Joy began, like she was responding to a silent question. She swallowed loudly.

"Joy. You don't have to—"

"It happened in the dark," she said in a rush, like the words were being ripped out of her. "It doesn't—I don't get the—the darkness doesn't trigger me every time, but sometimes—it's like I'm back there—and I can't—I *can't* ..."

Malachi twisted around slightly so he was facing her. He knew his red eyes could be startling in the darkness—he'd sent Desmond nearly flying out of his skin with fright, many a time—but Joy immediately met his glowing gaze like a drowning woman grasping at straws. She had to be struggling to see him in the darkness, but he could see her perfectly; her eyes were wide and scared, boring into his like his gaze was the blinking light of a lighthouse and she was a captain lost at sea, finally found home.

Malachi's hand inched forward in the space between them, shifting closer to her. The moment felt fragile, like he wasn't only reaching for her. When the tips of his fingers brushed hers, her hand moved abruptly, tangling their fingers together. Malachi suddenly couldn't breathe. She hadn't stopped staring into his eyes.

His heart thumped. "You're okay."

"I know." She didn't look away. Her hand squeezed his.

He scented more than saw her blush. "I don't know. I assumed demons were immortal?"

"We are."

"Oh. But ... you're ...?"

"I am very young, if you want to look at it that way, yes. But demons do not age like humans do. We are born already grown and self-sufficient, and learn about everything else in a relatively short amount of time."

"Ah." Her hands began to move again. Her breaths sped up as her fingers tangled in his curls, before touching the base of his horns. Her scent thickened. Malachi's mouth watered. "And you've never—no one's ever—?"

"No," Malachi gritted, as the tips of her fingers stroked over the grooves of his horns. "Never ... never like this."

"No one has touched you like this?" she asked in genuine surprise, like Malachi had people lining up who wanted to sweetly explore him like this; without any attachments, just for the simple pleasure of feeling him.

"Never like this," he admitted roughly.

"Just me?" Her scent went smoky, her voice husky with something that seemed almost possessive.

Malachi swallowed a sound. Fuck, he really liked the thought of that. He would very much like to be owned by Joy.

"Just you," he whispered.

Her hands moved down again, cupping his face, stroking down along his throat, lingering over the pulse at the base of his neck, before pressing flat against the planes of his chest.

"Okay?" she whispered.

"Please."

She trembled. "Darling."

Malachi trembled in turn. *Oh.* He had never given much thought to human sentiments beyond thinking they were vaguely sweet. But Joy calling him "darling"—it was almost as good as it had felt to consume the essence of Desmond's soul.

"You can touch me, too," Joy whispered.

His hands immediately moved to rest heavily on her thighs. "Thank you."

Joy trembled again. "Fuck, why does that turn me on so much?"

Malachi chuckled.

Joy shifted closer, then soft lips were pressing against a point directly underneath the side of his jaw. Malachi trembled all over. Joy kissed him again, her lips slightly parted so he felt the warm, damp brush of her tongue.

"Joy." He groaned.

She opened her mouth wider, lightly sinking her teeth into the side of his throat.

Malachi growled, his hands moving up to her hips, to the fleshy globes of her ass. Her skirt must've shifted when she'd adjusted her position, because it was now bunched over her hips. That meant the only thing separating Malachi's touch from her skin was the silky lace of her underwear.

Panting, she adjusted her position further until she was straddling his hips properly, then her lips were back on his jaw, her hands in his hair, drifting up until she was gripping the base of his horns.

Malachi grunted. His hips bucked, his grip on her ass tightening. Joy let out a soft cry, her hips rolling forward. He could feel the heat of her cunt through his robes—through the flimsy material of her underwear, and his dick *strained*.

The movement had brought her face closer to his, their breaths puffing against each other's mouths.

He abruptly fisted the short hair at the back of her head before his brain had finished processing the action, tilting her face and slanting his lips desperately over hers. Her lips were as soft as he'd imagined, her breaths rushed and hot.

Her mouth opened, and Malachi took the invitation, plunging his tongue into their hot depths. She moaned, wrapped her lips around the organ and *sucked*, making Malachi's hips jerk again. He began to thrust his tongue into her mouth, fucking into it, daring to slide even deeper, into her throat.

The movement of her hips grew frenzied, her grip on his horns making him see fucking stars. Without much thought, his robes abruptly parted so the thin material of her panties was the only barrier between them. The lips of her pussy were swollen and so fucking *slick*, parting around the girth of his dick, the heat of her cunt mercilessly teasing him with each rock of her hips.

Eventually, she had to pull back from the kiss to gasp. Saliva dripped from her chin and jaw as his tongue slid wetly out of her mouth. She was still gripping his horns, still rocking her hips, rolling them almost frantically, taking her pleasure.

"Fuck," Malachi snarled, digging his heels into the floor so he could move his hips into her thrusts.

"*Malachi*." She sobbed.

Malachi's hips jolted again, his thighs shaking. "*Fuck*." It wasn't his True Name, but he was his name all the same, and it felt like fucking ambrosia coming from her lips.

She shifted her hips, lifting them higher. It took him a moment to realise she must like the feeling of the ridges underneath his cockhead against her clit. With each rock of her hips—each perfect stroke—she let out a soft, mewling cry.

He had to bury his face in her shoulder, his mouth slack. His dick was fucking weeping. Her hands had left his horns— thank fucking Almighty—and were gripping his shoulders instead, her fingernails digging through his robes to his skin.

She leaned down and bit his shoulder. He could

practically taste her desperation.

"God—*Malachi*, please, *please*—"

He gripped her ass and hips in his hands, and took control. She willingly let go, crying out unabashedly into his throat as he moved her along his length, angling his hips so her clit rubbed against his straining dick just right.

"Yes," she gasped, "yes, yes, *yes*—"

Malachi bit his lip, bit the inside of his cheek, holding back his orgasm by the skin of his teeth.

She sat up suddenly and yanked her tank top and bra up, baring her breasts. Her hands went behind his head, pulling him down.

He greedily sucked one of her tits into his mouth, his tongue laving wetly over her stiff nipple, before he tugged gently on the sensitive bud with his teeth. She cried out, yanking his hair. His tail found its way out of his robes, curling around her other breast, the tip flicking hard against the hardened peak.

Joy's body locked up, and she came with an almost startled sounding cry, her thighs clamping around his hips, her pussy gushing between them. Malachi grunted, his eyes rolling back. His grip on her hips tightened painfully as he snapped his hips up frantically, selfishly using her satiated body as he strained to reach his own peak. It didn't take long; two more rolls of her hips and his expression was twisting with blissful agony as he followed her over the edge, his dick spilling hot and wet between them.

"Fuck. *Joy*."

She was limp against his chest, panting into his throat. "Oh my God," she said, her voice raspy.

He rocked her again, just a bit, to further milk the orgasm from his slowly softening dick. She jerked at the oversensitivity, but didn't move away.

"Jesus fucking Christ." She groaned.

The lights abruptly came on.

"Jesus fucking Christ," she repeated, burying her face in his throat.

Malachi felt terribly fond. Embarrassment spilled from Joy in waves.

"Joy."

"I'm not hiding," Joy said, her voice muffled into his throat.

Malachi sounded amused when he replied, "I didn't say you were."

His hands felt perfect on her hips, heavy and warm. She couldn't catalogue what he smelled like; it was something sweet and smoky, like apple-flavoured shisha, she thought hysterically. She pulled away after another moment to sit back on his thighs, meeting his eyes. He watched her, his red eyes practically boring into her soul. Then his eyes dipped.

Joy flushed when she remembered her tank top and bra were still bunched underneath her armpits, baring her breasts to the room, her nipples still hard. Malachi's expression darkened. To her right, his tail was out, flicking sharply in the air. Joy's cunt clenched when she remembered how it had felt flicking against the stiffness of her sensitive nipple.

She blushed as she tugged her tank top and bra down. Malachi's eyes lazily trailed up from her covered tits to meet her eyes.

"Hi," she said nonsensically, then prayed for the ground to open up and swallow her whole.

His lips twitched, even as he raised an eyebrow in confusion. "Hi."

They stared at each other. Joy's heart was thumping

weirdly. Her stomach was filled with dizzy, swarming butterflies.

She leaned down at the same time that he leaned up, and they were kissing again. The kiss was softer this time, exploring. It was her turn to nip at his lower lip with her blunt teeth; her turn to slide her tongue into his mouth. He moaned softly, parting his lips for her, letting her explore.

Joy pressed closer, wrapping her arms around his neck, tangling her fingers in his soft curls—kissing him like she never wanted to do anything else ever again.

They finally pulled apart to breathe, Joy resting her forehead against his. His hands had left her hips, and were now wrapped around her body, his palms pressed flat to her upper and lower back, spanning the entire length of it.

She was growing cold and uncomfortable between her legs, her underwear sticky with her arousal and earlier release, but she really, really didn't want to move. He was so warm. He felt so good.

Like he could read her mind, Malachi's hands on her back pressed gently, until Joy was fully lying down on top of him, her head resting on his shoulder.

"Okay?" he asked gruffly.

"Yes." Joy sighed.

She'd told herself to take several steps back, but instead, she'd run full-fucking-speed ahead. But what was she supposed to do? She'd had a mini-panic attack, he'd tried to calm her down, then he'd *touched* her—then *she* was touching *him*, and he'd confessed to not being touched in a long time, and she was just supposed to what? *Stop*?

Okay, maybe. Yes.

But then he'd kissed her, and Joy was lost.

She trembled with memory. Malachi's arms tightened around her in response, making her heart thump. Fuck, she didn't want to think about this right now. She knew she

abstract erotic paintings—adorned nearly all the walls. The talent had also seemed to "suddenly" surface after the death of her husband, which made her family feel even more justified in cutting her off.

She led them to the kitchen. Joy took a seat on one of six bar stools bracketing the kitchen island.

"What's your choice of soft drink?" Aunty Paloma asked, heading for the fridge. "Or do you prefer juice? Alcohol?"

"Just water's fine."

"No, you can't drink water. I made shawarmas earlier. They're in the oven. You're not allowed to say no."

Joy's lips twitched. "Then why ask?"

"I see that smart mouth of yours hasn't changed since." Aunty Paloma grinned.

Joy ducked her head. "Only with you."

Aunty Paloma laughed. "Go on, darling. Drink?"

She settled for orange juice, since Aunty Paloma said it had been freshly squeezed that morning. She couldn't resist some freshly made juice.

At first, they sat and ate and talked about nothing important. Joy appreciated the small talk, because it made her more confident to bring up why she'd really come here.

"So, you live here all by yourself?" Joy had wondered aloud two weeks ago.

There was a twinkle in her aunt's eye when she'd replied, *"Sure. You could say that."*

Joy had assumed perhaps her aunt had one-night stands, or a partner. It had been yet another reason the family had cut her off; her perpetual singleness and refusal to get married again—their words, not hers.

Now, Joy had a different suspicion.

"So." Aunty Paloma clapped her hands when they were done eating and had settled in the sitting room. "Shall we get to the crux of it? I know you're not just here to admire my décor. Have you done it, then?"

She asked it briskly, but calmly, like Joy summoning a demon to help her get away with murder was a normal occurrence.

"Not yet," Joy said, trying to mirror her aunt's calm and probably failing. "I actually came over because I have some questions."

Aunty Paloma raised both her eyebrows. "That couldn't be asked over the phone?"

"No." And risk the possibility of Malachi overhearing? Definitely fucking not. A text message wouldn't have sufficed, either; she needed to have this conversation face to face.

Her aunt huffed, waving a hand in a "go on" gesture.

"Do you have a contract with a demon?" She blurted it like ripping off a Band-Aid. She hadn't asked last time because she'd been terrified despite her resolve to go on with her plan.

Aunty Paloma was silent for a moment, watching her. Then her lips ticked up in the corner, and she said, "Of a sort."

Joy's heart leapt into her throat. She sat forward. "What does that mean?"

Aunty Paloma looked at her again—into her eyes, one after the other, like she was trying to gauge for herself if Joy was ready for this conversation.

Satisfied enough with what she saw, she said, "I sold my soul to kill my husband." Joy couldn't quite keep her eyes from bugging out. Aunty Paloma laughed. "Don't look so surprised. I was young and desperate, and Klaus was ... persuasive."

The way she said the demon's name made Joy shiver. It sounded familiar—*intimate*.

"Klaus is ..." Joy began, taking a sip of her juice to wet her suddenly dry throat.

"My demon, yes," Aunty Paloma finished.

"*Your—*" Joy sputtered, quickly snapping her mouth shut, her cheeks on fire.

Aunty Paloma's lips ticked up again. "Your demon must be pretty persuasive, too. Is that why you're here?"

She thought of sitting in Malachi's lap last night, his hands on her hips rocking her against his dick. Then afterward, when they'd fucking *cuddled* on the sofa and watched TV until the sun had come up. Who knew Malachi was also a big fan of cartoons, even though he tried to do something as ridiculously endearing as try to make sense of their randomness.

"He literally died in the last scene," Malachi had complained when Anton, the character who was literally a piece of toast, had been eaten by a flock of seagulls, but appeared in the next scene, hale and hearty. "How is he here again, alive and well? And they're acting like everything is normal, when they were *there*."

"Please, stop," Joy had said, laughing so hard her stomach hurt. Malachi had seemed to like making her laugh, exaggerating his questions and complaints until Joy was nearly peeing herself with it.

Joy's lips almost twitched at the memory. Fuck. If it weren't for her dark skin, she'd probably be as red as a ripe strawberry.

"That's not—he's not—I was just curious. I didn't sell my soul," she tacked on, like it would make her look less guilty.

"And now you *want* to sell your soul?" Aunty Paloma looked confused.

"What? No." Joy blushed again. "I was just—I was curious. On whether you had a contract or not. I wasn't brave enough to ask last time. That's literally it."

Aunty Paloma stared at her, seeing right through her bullshit. "You don't need my permission to fuck your demon, Joy."

"Jesus fucking Christ, Aunty." Joy wanted the ground to open up and swallow her.

"Or perhaps you'd rather date them?" Aunty Paloma said, wagging her eyebrows. "That *is* why you're here, isn't it?"

"*No*," Joy said, mortified.

Aunty Paloma was enjoying her embarrassment way too much.

Her smile didn't fade as she said, "I can introduce you to Klaus sometime, if you want."

Joy's heart began to pound. She tried not to look too eager. "He's here? In the mortal realm, I mean."

"Yes. And Klaus uses "they/them", please. I'd introduce them now, but they usually take a walk around this time and won't be back for at least another hour." Aunty Paloma's nose wrinkled. "I can't believe I found them attractive at all; they're so obsessed with walking and nature and exercise and "healthy" meals. It's exhausting."

Joy's lip twitched. Her aunt sounded long-suffering, but the fond smile curving her lips said otherwise. Then Joy's heart returned to pounding when what they were talking about properly sank in.

Her aunt was dating a demon. And by the looks of it, it had been going on for at least the past fifteen years, since Aunty Paloma had gotten rid of her husband.

What the fuck is even going on?

"You *would* like to meet them, right?" Aunty Paloma asked, raising an eyebrow.

Joy nodded quickly. "Yeah. Okay. Yes. I'd love that."

Her aunt smiled knowingly. Joy didn't think she'd ever blushed this much in her life. She had a lot more questions to ask, but was too embarrassed now to ask them. She didn't want her aunt getting any ideas. She was just here for ... research purposes.

"Good luck with the rest of your revenge," Aunty Paloma said, walking her to the door after she'd called a Bolt. "Call me when you're done so you can update me on how it goes. I'll talk to Klaus, and we'll discuss a date you can meet them."

"Right. Thank you, Aunty."

"And don't be a stranger, you hear?"

"Yes, Aunty."

Joy waved. Her aunt watched her until the Bolt disappeared down the curved road. Joy turned back to face her front, ignoring her pounding heart.

Her heart didn't stop racing until she was back in her little accommodation, the treacherous organ leaping damnably into her throat when she spotted Malachi, as usual, dwarfing the sofa, a small, cute frown on concentration on his face as he watched the TV. He could be so still, sometimes, almost like a shadow.

He glanced at her when she stood there staring for too long. "How was your visit with your aunt?" he asked, smiling.

Joy wanted to go over there and climb into his lap for no reason other than the pleasure of doing so. She felt ... sheltered, when he held her. Small. Safe. She knew she could get addicted to the feeling, which was the only thing that stopped her.

"The visit was—fine," she strangled out. "I'm—I need to ... pee."

Malachi's eyebrow twitched. "Are you asking for my permission?"

"Shut up." Malachi huffed out an amused breath. Joy's cheeks were on fire. Oh God.

She disappeared into the bathroom. Turned the tap on. Wet her face and slapped her cheeks. She stared at her reflection. Fuck, her eyes were so bright, so obviously hungry.

She didn't think she'd needed her aunt's permission, but she'd gotten it anyway.

Joy was going to fuck Malachi. Oh, she was absolutely going to fuck him. She clenched her thighs together, remembering how it had felt to grind against the ridged head of his dick—the oh-so-fucking brain-circuiting feel of it had nearly had her drooling and losing her mind.

She *had* to fuck him.

It didn't have to mean anything. After what her rapist had done to her, why shouldn't Joy take pleasure where she saw fit? She hadn't thought she'd ever feel or even accept this kind of pleasure since that day, and she didn't know if it was a fluke or just ... Malachi.

As for everything else—the way he made her laugh, how hungry she was to know everything about him; what made *him* laugh?—she couldn't entertain any of that.

This had to be about fucking only. Fucking was easy. Simple. Uncomplicated. After everything, Joy desperately *needed* easy, simple, and uncomplicated. Anything more was going to be too much.

Besides, she couldn't really date a demon, no matter what her aunt thought. Right? No, that was fucking ridiculous. How would it even work? Would she be able to introduce him to Iyore? Or take him out on dates, or whatever? Probably not.

"Stop thinking about dating him," Joy whisper-growled

at her reflection.

She thought of Malachi admitting how he hadn't been touched, probably since he'd been fifteen years old, and felt her heart give a weird little jolt. He'd let her touch him—he'd let her—he'd wanted her—he loves *cartoons*, for fuck's sake—

"It doesn't mean anything," she said stubbornly.

One night, she told herself. She'd have one night, their contract would end, and Joy would go back to her life, ready to start rebuilding the pieces her rapist had crumbled, hopefully leaving the demon and the entirety of this surreal interlude of her life behind her forever.

NINE

Malachi watched Joy with barely concealed hunger when she exited the bathroom in nothing but a flimsy little white towel. She smirked at him when she noticed him staring, and didn't reprimand him when he adjusted his position on the sofa so he could continue staring at her.

She didn't close the netting when she took a seat on her bed after retrieving a container of moisturiser from her windowsill. His lower belly turned molten as he watched her massage the cocoa-buttery cream onto her skin until it melted and shone. She stroked it onto her long, shapely legs; up her thick, soft arms.

She stood and turned around so her back was to him. Then she dropped the towel.

Malachi sucked in a sharp breath. Holy shit. Joy glanced at him from over her shoulder, her lips tugged up into a pleased little smirk. Fucking Almighty. She moisturised the rest of her body, practically caressing herself. Malachi was about to swallow his tongue.

Tonight was the night. Malachi shoved down the panic trying to smother his senses. His contract with Joy was soon coming to an end. He really didn't want to think about it. Not now. Not yet.

He watched her, instead, as she slid on her underwear— soft, white satin—up her legs, settling them on her wide hips. Her bra followed, then she put on her blood red dress splattered with white. She combed her hair, did her face, and finally slid her feet into her heels.

She'd painted her nails earlier, the same blood red as her outfit. Her dagger lay in wait for her on top of the small kitchen counter.

She picked it up and turned to face Malachi, her aura bright and blinding.

Malachi shook with want. It was too soon. Their contract couldn't end—not yet. He *wanted*—Almighty, he'd never wanted so much. Just another day. Another week. There was so much possibility between them. He needed to know where —how far—it could take them. How could he taste something so sweet, feel something so good, only for it to end so abruptly? He couldn't. He couldn't.

But he was too afraid to ask.

All his life, there'd only been a single time Malachi had ever asked for anything.

It had been to the Priest, the first time Malachi had broken. He'd begged if not to free him, then to at least let him feed.

"I won't run," he'd pleaded, young and vulnerable, and oh so naïve, "I won't try to escape or cheat the sect. Just please —please—just let me ..."

The Priest had disregarded his plea like he hadn't spoken at all, emotionlessly reciting the words to the spell that would rip Malachi from hell to the mortal realm, where a gullible human willing to sell their soul waited.

The thought of Joy doing the same thing—of her expression twisting into a disgusted sneer if he tried to form the words kept Malachi from speaking. They'd barely spent three days in each other's company. His research of human companionship told him it could be sometimes fickle and unpredictable, and other times, overwhelming but grounding. But the general consensus was that it would probably be really fucking creepy for him to ask after only three days.

Why would she even want a demon? Of course, Malachi had come across other demons—probably escaped nicquiris, like he was—trawling the earth, but he'd kept clear of them just in case they were sentries in disguise.

But now, he wondered. What if they were here by choice? What if they had contracts that bound them to the mortal realm—to a human, for the rest of their natural lives? The thought made his heart thump with yearning.

But could he ask that of Joy? It felt like too much, too soon.

"Are you ready, demon boy?" Joy's expression was hard, determined.

Malachi wanted to kiss her. "Ready when you are, little tiger."

Joy held out her arm. Malachi slid his palm into the dip of her elbow, holding her gently. They took a step, and the world blurred around them, morphing into the sitting room of the man they'd been terrorising.

They were a little later than usual, which Joy had wanted. She'd wanted her victim to be asleep when she finally finished him off.

Joy located the stairs, and she and Malachi made their way up. She guessed where the man's bedroom was based on the layout of the house on the first try.

They didn't need to sneak, Malachi's abilities lending them the stealth of a predator in the night.

The man was indeed asleep, spread eagle on top of his sheets.

Joy's lip curled with disgust as she watched him. "I wish I could haunt him in his dreams like he's been haunting mine," she whispered, words vicious. "How perfect would it be when he wakes up, thinking he's safe, only to see me standing right here in his bedroom?"

Fuck, Malachi wanted her so fucking much.

"We can do that," he said, voice gruff, glancing at her.

Joy looked sharply at him. Her grip on her dagger tightened. "You can go into his dreams?"

"The dreamscape is a part of the Veil," Malachi said. "All nicquiris can traverse it." It had been one of the many ways the Priest had had him find gullible humans willing to sell their soul to a demon.

"Delicious." Joy's lips stretched. She turned her focus back on the sleeping man, her expression and her scent doing serious things to Malachi's libido. "Let's do it."

The man was dreaming of what seemed to be his secondary school. The scene was fuzzy in the way some dreams were, but the man was in the middle, surrounded by friends, having a conversation that didn't make sense, as these dreams often didn't.

"What would you like to do?" Malachi whispered.

They were hidden within the man's dreamscape, thanks to Malachi's powers.

"Can you only travel the dreamscape? Or can you ...

manipulate it?"

"I can manipulate it to an extent," Malachi said. "But it is easier for me if the dream has some relation to their actual life." That way, the human's subconscious automatically took control.

Joy grinned. "That's perfect."

After Joy told him what she wanted, Malachi closed his eyes and pulled from the aether. It took a lot more power to manipulate the dreamscape, but for her, Malachi was beginning to realise he would do anything.

He opened his eyes, and they were standing in the bar, exactly as Joy had described. Joy's clothes had changed; she was dressed in plain blue jeans, a pink t-shirt with her favourite cartoon on it, and plain grey sneakers.

Joy slipped into her role in the dream easily, heading to the bar and ordering a drink from the nondescript person behind it.

The man's subconscious remembered this moment in reality, of course, grasping at Malachi's direction with rapt eagerness. Malachi saw the corner of Joy's lips curl up, like she knew it, too.

The man was staring hungrily at Joy sitting alone at the bar, ignoring the rest of their co-workers as they cracked jokes and got increasingly drunk. He moved closer to her, his expression melting into something innocent.

Malachi's stomach felt rotten, curdled like spoilt milk.

Joy was the perfect actress as her victim sidled up to her, saying something that made her laugh shyly. Malachi wondered if this was how it had happened. He syphoned more power from the aether so Joy could slip something into the man's drink.

The man saw it happen, clear as day. Malachi watched him frown, the lights in the dreamscape dimming. But despite this, he still took the drink, his subconscious

overlaying the moment with what had happened in reality—
that it had been the other way round.

The dreamscape flickered, the scene changed, and they
were in an unfamiliar flat. Malachi bit back a snarl when he
saw that the man was on top of Joy, even though this had
been part of Joy's plan.

He clenched his jaw and practically yanked from the
aether. Their roles abruptly switched, and Joy was the one
on top. She sat back in the man's lap, grinning ferally down
at him.

He smiled up at her, but his expression seemed slightly
confused.

"Something wrong, pretty boy?" Joy asked sultrily,
stroking her hands down his chest.

He tried to move, his eyes widening with alarm when he
found that he couldn't. Malachi felt drunk on the heady
scent of Joy's viciousness.

"What—?" His mouth clicked shut when he realised Joy
was abruptly holding a dagger. "What? Joy—what are you
doing? What's going on? Let me go!"

"No."

She swung the dagger down.

They were abruptly ejected from the dreamscape as Joy's
victim shot awake in the real world, crying out and clutching
his chest. He didn't notice Joy and Malachi—not yet,
collapsing back onto his mattress, panting hard.

Joy gripped her dagger hard, waiting, waiting. She
watched as he reached underneath the pillows for his phone
and checked the time. Then he fell back onto his bed.

Joy silently counted.

Three.

Two.

The man's eyes darted to the darkest corner of his room, where Malachi and Joy stood, silent like shadows. Of course, Malachi was only visible to her—this wasn't about him. But Joy could tell *he* could see her in the darkness; a hint of her bloody red dress.

He practically leapt up from his bed, reaching frantically for the light switch. He jolted, flying backward when Joy didn't disappear. Malachi remained invisible.

Joy took a step forward. Her blade glinted. Her heart raced, but not with fear.

With power.

"Hello, rapist."

He jolted again. "W-What's this? What's—?" He was beginning to sweat.

"W-What—w-what ..." Joy mocked. "Cat got your tongue?"

"How the fuck did you get inside my house?" He quickly slid out of his bed, like if he stood, he'd gain some of the advantage. "What the fuck do you—?" he continued angrily.

"Aht-aht." Like Malachi was an extension of her already, he made a motion through the air and the man was abruptly silenced. "I don't want to hear a word you have to say. I don't even want to hear you beg, though that would be nice."

He stumbled backward. Joy advanced on him, a predator stalking her prey.

He kept trying to speak, but the words refused to leave his mouth. When Joy's blade glinted again, she heard the sound of something splashing, before the acrid smell of urine reached her nose.

Joy wrinkled her nose with disgust, even as her lips curled with manic pleasure.

"Seriously? Is this really all it takes?"

He tried to speak again. Once more, like Malachi could read her mind, the man's body was abruptly moving without his control, forcing him onto the bed until he was lying flat on his back.

Joy climbed onto the bed, spreading her feet apart so she was balanced on her heels.

She stared down at him, remembering how she'd cried and begged. How she'd pleaded, and then, when she realised it was futile, she'd abruptly stopped fighting.

Oh, how he'd *hated* that. He'd wanted her to claw and scream. He'd slapped her. Gripped her jaw, hitting her again when she closed her eyes. He'd forced her to watch, her jaw clenched, tears slipping down her temples.

Those tears filled her eyes now. She remembered how she'd had to lay there in the darkness afterward, unable to move because of the drugs still running rampant through her system. Her unlocked door—her empty flat—her heart had never pounded so hard; she'd never felt so exposed. So violated. So *afraid*, some part of her waiting for him to come back—maybe someone would come in after him; maybe he'd bring his friends.

Her panic had forced her into an exhausted sleep, only for her to be haunted by hallucinations of him—of the incident occurring over and over again.

By the time she'd regained some strength, forcing herself to crawl and lock her door, all her emotions had shut down. Calling the police would have been useless. She'd thought of calling Iyore, but even though it hadn't been her fault, she'd still felt ashamed.

She should've been paying more attention. She should have said no when her co-workers asked if she wanted to go to the bar for a small breather, as she always did.

She should've refused his help when he'd looked so *concerned* when she suddenly couldn't seem to stand straight as the night wore on. She'd thought he was her friend. She'd thought she could trust him to get her home safely when she was so vulnerable.

She should've—she should've—she should've.

Joy dropped to her knees, her thighs spread wide over his. He was shaking, his chest heaving with silent sobs.

"Disgusting." She sneered. "Fucking pitiful."

He was dressed only in his briefs.

Joy pressed the tip of her dagger against his upper belly. Slowly, with barely half the amount of pressure she'd expected, the blade sank into his stomach.

He seized up, his mouth parted in a silent scream.

Joy remembered how she'd tried to move on. She'd quit her job, changed her number, and moved out of her flat. She'd tried looking for a new job, tried putting the pieces of her shattered self back together, but it felt like with every piece she picked up, ten more cracked and broke off.

She'd fallen into a depression. Bouts of moments where she called herself weak for not just *getting over it*. She'd tried to have sex with someone new—a woman instead of a man, as if that would have made a difference—and nearly vomited on her when she'd looked at Joy with that intent in her eyes.

Then had come the anger. She wondered what he was doing, while she was here, spiralling.

Turned out life had simply gone on for him. Nothing had changed.

Joy had known then, there was only one of two ways this was going to end.

With her death.

Or with his.

Joy pulled out the blade. Blood spilled from the wound. She pressed it in again in a fresh new spot, slow and easy. He was shouting, but his body remained perfectly still and quiet, thanks to Malachi.

TEN

Malachi slid his hands underneath her knees and lifted her legs up, hooking them over his broad shoulders.

"I'm still—my heels," Joy gasped breathlessly, even as her cunt clenched and her pussy warmed, growing wet.

"Leave them on," he said roughly.

Her lower belly swooped. "*Fuck*. Okay." He gripped her hips and abruptly tugged her right to the edge of the mattress so her cunt was right in his face, forcing her to lean back to balance the rest of her body on her elbows. "Oh my God."

His hands went to the band of her skirt, and he tugged impatiently.

Joy nodded quickly. "Yes. You can—"

He tore the skirt off her hips. He ripped her panties off next.

"Fuck." Joy laughed breathlessly. She'd never gotten so

wet so fast in her life. "I didn't say you could go for the panties. Those were fucking silk."

"I'll make you an identical pair," Malachi gruffed, leaning over her, spreading her thighs wider.

Before Joy could think of a witty retort, his mouth was on her. Her eyes rolled back. She lost her balance, falling flat onto the mattress, her hips jolting up into that sinful heat. He parted his lips around her throbbing clit, and sucked.

"*Malachi.*" She moaned, reaching down to grab his horns, keeping him there.

He grunted, opening his mouth wider, his deliciously slick tongue splitting apart her pussy lips like a hot knife to butter. He lapped hungrily at her dripping cunt like he was laving the juices off a fruit, before his mouth was wrapping around her clit and sucking again.

Joy arched, crying out. She tugged desperately on his horns. "Oh God. Please, please, please—"

He sucked on her clit until she was seeing fucking stars; harsh, deep pulls that almost felt too fucking much. Her thighs clamped around his head, her hips lifting higher and higher, her thighs beginning to shake.

The pressure and the rhythm were so fucking acute—practically on the edge of painful—Joy could feel it from her clit to her stiff, sensitive nipples—from her toes all the way to the tips of her fucking hair.

"Oh my God," she cried when she felt the orgasm building, deep in her gut. It felt too much. She tried to squirm away, her thighs vibrating, her toes curling. "Fuck, fuck, *Malachi*—I'm—"

Her mind went blank. She went silent and still as she came, explosions going off in her brain.

"*Fuck.*" She sobbed, rocking her hips up desperately into his face, grinding her clit into his mouth, trying to prolong the orgasm. "Fuck. Fuck. Oh my fucking God." She couldn't stop shaking.

Malachi had eased off, but he hadn't stopped, gently licking her as she came down from her orgasm, her body going limp.

He turned his face to kiss the inside of her thigh, his voice a sexy timbre when he said, "You smell so fucking good. Taste so fucking good."

"Fuck." Joy sighed, her brain still a pile of mush.

"Can you come again?"

"*Fuck*." Joy's cunt clenched.

"That's not a no." She glanced down to see him smirking at her, before he put his mouth on her cunt once more.

"Jesus *Christ*."

The tip of his tongue swirled over her clit, sending her hips jolting at the oversensitivity, before he was suddenly thrusting the slick length of it inside her.

His grip on her hips were the only thing that kept her from flying off the mattress.

His tongue began to pump inside her, filling her even better than she'd imagined in her dream.

"*Yes*!" she hissed, her voice holding a hint of a growl. "Fuck, yes, oh my God—make me come, make me come, make me come—"

Malachi groaned, and did exactly as he was told. He curled his tongue inside her so it hit all the right spots, not slowing down his thrusts until Joy was shaking again.

Her legs abruptly locked around his head, her heels digging into his wings, her hands practically yanking on his horns as she came again, her cunt spasming so hard his tongue was forced out of her. The moment it slipped out, she proceeded to squirt all over his face.

"H-Holy shit." Her voice sounded scratchy. Fuck, had she been screaming? "H-Holy *fucking* shit."

Malachi moved. He gripped her hips, then tugged her

easily up the bed until she was lying in the middle of it, before he practically fell on top of her, desperately joining their mouths.

Joy tangled her fingers in his soft curls, kissing him back just as desperately. The taste of her cunt in his mouth lit her up from inside out, had her gripping his hair more tightly, kissing him so hard her teeth pressed painfully against the inside of her lips.

She spread her thighs wide so he could settle properly between them. His robes must have disappeared at some point, because all she could feel was soft, smooth skin. Groaning, Joy hungrily ran her hands up his bare back, across his broad shoulders, over his muscled arms. Her hands found his wings, sinking into his soft, fluffy feathers. The sound he made when she tugged on them went straight to her cunt.

Malachi abruptly broke the kiss with a lewd sounding smack and sat up, forcing her to let go of his wings. His hands found the edge of her top, grasping, then he ripped it off, flinging the torn pieces across the room. He slid a claw underneath the strap of her bra between her breasts, and tore it neatly in two.

Joy's breasts happily spilled out of their confinements. She felt so fucking wanton now, dressed in nothing but her heels, and tatters of her white, lace bra.

"Jesus." She squirmed. "You fucking animal."

He grinned, his smile edged with a hint of fang. "You don't smell so upset."

"Stop smelling me."

He laughed, cupping her tits, stroking his thumbs over her stiff nipples. Joy moaned, arching into the touch. Her stomach swarmed with wild butterflies at the sound of his laughter. Had she ever heard him laugh before? She wanted to make him laugh again. He leaned down to take one of her breasts into his mouth, sucking gently, laving her sensitive nipple with his tongue, and all thoughts flew from her head.

"Malachi," she whined.

He made an encouraging sound around her breast, slightly increasing the pressure, scraping sharp teeth over the peak and sending her breath hissing sharply out of her.

He adjusted his position on top of her, parting her thighs wider and shifting his hips until his stiff length came in contact with her cunt.

"Fuck." He pulled back from her tit, his mouth slack, rocking his hips messily, gliding his dick through her excessive wetness. "*Fuck.*"

His desperation was like a fucking aphrodisiac. She'd come twice, yet here she was, ready to fucking go again.

"Yeah, come on," she begged, gripping his hair, rolling her hips into the stuttered grind of his own. "Do it, Malachi." She wanted him to fill her right fucking now—so much she couldn't think. "Fuck me, fuck me—"

Malachi's head felt like it was swamped in fog. All he could see, breathe, and feel was Joy. She was so fucking wet, the sinful glide of her pussy along his length short-circuiting his brain.

"Fuck me." She was begging. "Please, please—come on, Malachi, fuck me, fuck me—"

Panting, desperate, his dick fucking *dripping*, he balanced on one elbow, reaching between them so he could aim his prick at her cunt. She spread those soft, lush thighs wider, lifting her hips slightly, giving him better access.

He froze just before he made contact with her flesh. "Fuck. Protection?"

Joy shook her head quickly. "I'm STD-free, last time I checked. And I literally can't get pregnant." She knocked on her lower belly like it was an empty container. "No uterus." She waggled her eyebrows. Her expression and her scent made his lips twitch; she sounded so pleased about it. "Debilitating fibroids when I was twenty-one," she explained when she noticed his curiosity. "Decided to just get rid of the whole thing since I'm not interested in having children."

Malachi nodded. "I can use my magic to make sure I'm safe, and I've never been with anyone," he added in a rush.

Joy's eyes widened. "What? Really? No one? Ever?" She squirmed; her scent went dark, smoky with possessiveness.

Fucking Almighty. "Yes."

"Okay. Fuck. Come here." He leaned down, and she kissed him—soft and sweet; slow and deep. "Okay, I'm ready—you can—"

Malachi pressed forward. He couldn't suppress his moan when the head of his dick came in contact with her slick opening. He had to stop for a second, had to take a moment to breathe. Almighty, she was so fucking *wet*; so hot and slick. He pressed harder against her, stars bursting behind his eyelids as her pussy slowly opened up for the head of his dick.

Malachi's other hand clawed at the mattress. His lower belly was quivering. He was going really fucking slowly, his muscles nearly cramping from the effort it was taking to not just cram his entire length into her.

She managed to take the tapered head, but her body refused to take any more. He shifted his legs, trying to change the angle, but the sharp scent of pain immediately halted him.

"I'm hurting you."

"Only—only a little bit," Joy admitted breathlessly, in the same tone of someone announcing the weather.

The laugh that burst out of him was entirely unexpected. Joy laughed, too, giggling into his chest.

"Joy." Fuck, the scent of her right now. Malachi wanted to bottle it so he could have it on his person forever. "We should—"

"No," Joy said desperately, sensing that he wanted to stop. "Just—just go slowly, yeah?"

Breathing hard, Malachi tried to push in again. It wasn't going to work; Joy had tensed up in the anticipation of pain, and Malachi really didn't want to hurt her.

"Joy—"

"Keep going."

"Don't be so stubborn."

"If you don't get your fucking dick inside me, so help me God—"

Malachi laughed, his heart aching. "Joy."

"Don't you fucking stop, I mean it," she growled, her voice nearly a sob. "Please. I want it. I can take it."

Malachi bit his lip. His dick jerked in his grip, eking out more streams of pre-come. *Fuck*. Using every ounce of control he could muster to keep himself still, he slid his tail between them. His hand left his dick to hold onto her hip.

"Oh, *oh*." She gasped, his grip keeping her from flying out of position as the tip of his tail stroked against her no-doubt oversensitive clit. "Holy fuck. Jesus fucking Christ."

He didn't stop, roughly circling her clit, fast and hard, until her body began to lock up. The opening of her cunt spasmed wildly around the head of his prick, nearly driving him out of his fucking mind.

"Joy," he snarled, barely clinging to a thread. "*Come*."

"*Malachi*." She did as she was told, the orgasm short and hard and no less intense. "Oh my God, Malachi. I'm fucking dying. Holy shit."

He held her as she shook. When she finally came down,

her cunt had relaxed enough that he could sink his dick in a little further.

Malachi's eyes watered. He pulled out an inch, then sank in again, her cunt managing to take more of him. Biting his lip hard, he did it again—then again and again, her body taking more and more of him with each little thrust, until he was buried to the hilt.

"Fuck." He had to take a moment to get used to the feel of her tight little cunt absolutely throttling the fuck out of his dick. "*Uhn*. Almighty. Fuck. *Fuck*." He rolled his hips, shaky and desperate, the slick, clenching grip of her pussy like nothing he'd ever felt.

It seemed that Joy had lost her ability to speak. Her mouth was wide open, her eyelashes fluttering, her nails digging into his back. She had let her thighs fall completely open, and she lay limp, completely relaxed, practically drooling as he began to speed up, pumping into her.

Malachi bit his lower lip viciously. She was just fucking *taking* it—letting out these sweet little sounds with each harsh slap of his hips.

His eyes watered. She smelled so fucking good right now, like pleasure and sex and something else, something that had his hips slamming even faster, harder.

"Oh God." She gulped. There were tears sliding down her temples, but Malachi knew they were tears of overwhelm, not of pain or upset. Her hands had moved into his hair, gripping his horns in tight fists. The edge of her heels scraped against the back of his thighs, adding an extra bite of sensation to their embrace. "Oh my God, Malachi." Her voice was a low, sobbing whine.

Too fucking soon, he could feel it building, starting deep in the base of his spine, in the heat of his belly. He bit the inside of his cheek, trying to hold back, to prolong it, but he couldn't, he couldn't.

He managed to frantically shove his tail between her legs as his thighs began to shake, aiming for her clit.

"No." Joy's voice was a wheeze. She slapped his tail away, yanking him down so he was lying fully on top of her. "It's your turn, now, darling." She gripped the base of his wings, the part where they protruded from his back. "Come on, come on—fill me up—fill me—"

Malachi's vision went white. He cried out, gasping raggedly as he came, so hard it felt like he'd died a little. His wings flared, blanketing the bed.

"Fuck. Joy." He rolled his hips, mouth slack, pumping her full. Joy weakly clenched the muscles of her cunt, trying to milk him. "*Joy*," he whined, arching, shaking, his voice cracked.

He sank on top of her when it was over, exhaling long and slow, his face pressed into her collarbone.

Joy's hands slid from his wings to the middle of his back, below his shoulder blades. She smelled like pleasure, contentment, and sweet exhaustion. When his softening dick slid out of her, her entire body vibrated in a sweet, little shiver, and she let out a soft sigh as his release spilled out of her afterward, staining her thighs and the sheets. She seemed to like the feeling—which was fucking hot—so Malachi did nothing to get rid of the mess just yet.

She was so soft and so warm all over; Malachi wished he never had to move again. Like she agreed with the sentiment, she said nothing about his weight possibly crushing her, simply breathing deep and slow, her hands tracing patterns across his back.

They lay there like that for Malachi didn't know how long, their breaths slowing, the sweat on their bodies rapidly cooling, while Malachi's heart pounded a discordant rhythm. He clenched his eyes shut, like it'd suppress the emotions rapidly building inside him. He could fall asleep like this, and he never fucking slept.

Then Joy spoke, her voice nothing more than a breath, "I could eat an entire cow right now."

Despite himself, Malachi burst out laughing.

ELEVEN

Joy grinned, her heart somersaulting and her belly fluttering madly at the sound of Malachi's unrestrained laughter.

He shifted, lifting his body off her so he was balanced on his elbows, staring down at her. Joy instantly missed the grounding warmth of his weight on hers. She should've felt vulnerable like this, naked underneath him, her thighs still spread around his hips, her feet still in her heels. Instead, she felt unusually sexy. Powerful. She slowly trailed her fingers up his back, feeling out the taut shapes of his muscles, enjoying his little shiver at her exploration.

"What'll you like, then?" His voice was gruff; his red eyes twinkled.

That fluttery feeling in her stomach intensified. She raised an eyebrow. "You can cook?"

He shrugged, his dark wings shrugging with him. Something about the way they blanketed the bed had Joy tingling between her thighs, her tender pussy eager for round two.

"In a sense."

Joy's eyes narrowed. She was curious, and really fucking hungry, though, so she took some time to really think about it.

"Anything," Malachi murmured, his eyes on hers. Something about his tone—the seriousness of it—had that fluttery feeling in her stomach intensifying once more. "Anything you want."

"A double cheeseburger," Joy decided, snapping her fingers, her mouth watering. When last had she had a burger? "Curly fries. Chocolate milkshake. And a chicken shawarma for dessert." She waggled her eyebrows.

Malachi laughed. He moved, making to sit up, resting on his knees. Joy sat up as well, blinking when Malachi waved a hand and the sticky mess staining their thighs and the sheets abruptly disappeared. Her feet had somehow been relieved of her heels, which she could see were now in the corner with her other shoes.

Joy pulled the now clean sheets—they smelled familiar, like something sweet but smoky—was that his magic?—into her lap just for something to do with her hands.

"A double cheeseburger, curly fries, chocolate milkshake, and a chicken shawarma; coming right up," Malachi murmured.

She expected Malachi to leave the bed. Instead, his eyes glowed blindingly bright, forcing her to look away. When she looked back, there was a steaming tray in her lap with all the items she'd requested. The tray was the plain grey of a cafeteria tray. The food items could've been from any fast-food restaurant given their distinct yellow, red, and white packaging.

"Um, what the fuck."

Malachi looked smug. The scent from the burger and the shawarma made Joy's stomach rumble loudly. Malachi's lip curled in the corners, revealing a hint of fang. Christ, he was so handsome.

Joy tore into the packaging for the burger. She brought it to her drooling mouth, then paused. "Wait, can I actually eat this? You didn't, like, make this from the waters in the depths of hell or something?"

Malachi chuckled, but he looked a bit disgusted. "No, don't be ridiculous. I happened to have all the ingredients in my pantry; I simply manipulated the aether to ... "cook" the meal, shall we say."

Joy blinked. Fuck. She'd nearly forgotten he had a house here. Well, in the mortal realm, not specifically *here*, in Arehjia. A new spark of curiosity lit up in her stomach. She wondered what his house was like.

She'd already decided she wanted to see it before the thought could even finish forming.

Filled with a new determination, Joy began to eat like an animal, uncaring of her audience. Malachi's eyes flared, and her TV came on. Fuck, should she be finding it hot that he could do magic like that?

The TV acted as some background noise as she practically demolished the food in record time, then slipped out of the bed as she began to sip from her milkshake. Excitement made her pulse thud. Did he live in an actual house? A flat? A ramshackle hut? Or in a castle? Despite how unlikely it probably was, she really hoped it was the latter.

She paused when she reached for her wardrobe, suddenly spinning around to face him as reality came crashing down on her.

Wait. What was she doing? Wasn't their contract over? Why was he still here? Was he waiting for her to kick him out? Did she *want* to kick him out? Joy's heart leapt into her throat when she realised she wasn't sure if she wanted to. Not now. Not yet.

But could he really stay here forever, if she never said a word about it? She didn't know if she liked that thought very much, either.

She spun back to face the wardrobe, her heartbeat going haywire.

"Is our contract over, then?" she asked, deliberately trying to sound light and breezy and like she didn't give a single fuck.

Malachi's gaze on her made the spot between her shoulder blades prickle.

"Not yet," he said, after a tiny pause that could have filled the river Niger. Joy hated the relief that flooded her, so intense it left her weak-kneed. "I have not yet completed my end of our bargain; to make your revenge look like an accident."

Right. Right. That was true. She supposed that meant he had to go back to do something with the body. Make it less bloody; remove all evidence of her presence and all that. Maybe use his magic to stage a break-in? Or was he going to make it look more natural, like a heart attack?

Whatever he did, it meant that as long as he didn't fulfil his end of the bargain, their contract remained.

And so did he.

Joy's stomach squirmed with emotions she refused to unpack. She began to rifle determinately through her wardrobe. This was going to end at some point, but before that did, Joy was going to satisfy her curiosity.

After this was all over, she was going to do what she'd planned to do after she'd finished enacting her revenge; rebuild her life, and resume living instead of merely surviving.

Malachi couldn't be a part of that plan, no matter what her foolish heart thought.

Malachi had no idea what was going on. When Joy had put on a t-shirt and jogging bottoms that frankly had no business hugging all her curves like that, she'd placed her hands on her hips and practically demanded to see his house.

Malachi hadn't been able to deny those eyes, that pursed mouth—not that he'd even wanted to—so, he'd simply taken her elbow and marched them through the aether.

"Malachi," Joy said when they rematerialized.

Malachi felt his lips twitch.

Joy turned to look at him, her expression twisted with dismay. "This is a forest," she said.

Malachi couldn't hold it any longer, he laughed. Joy's eyes lit up at the sound, though she still looked confused.

"Do demons and humans have different concepts of what a "house" is?"

Malachi laughed again. God, her scent when he laughed. He reached out, and she easily tangled their fingers together, the action ruining him completely.

"Come on," he said gruffly.

Strangely, he felt nervous. He had wards placed around his house at about a thousand metre radius into the surrounding wilderness, which was why he couldn't appear directly in front of it when he went through the aether.

Malachi felt gratified when Joy hissed under her breath, "*Yes*," her scent bursting bright with elation when they finally spotted his abode.

"You live in a fucking *castle*," Joy continued, voice awed. "God is real."

Malachi bit his lower lip, fondness spreading underneath his breast.

She let go of his hand so she could race up the wide, marble staircase leading to the front doors. She spun around when she was at the top.

"Okay, not to say we don't have castles in Nigeria, but what the fuck. There's no way this was here when you found it."

"It was not," Malachi confirmed, lips twitching.

Her eyes grew ten times wider, reminding him of a puppy pleading for snacks. "Did you ... did you *build* it yourself?" she asked, her voice breathy.

"Yes," Malachi said, though it had taken up a lot of magic. He'd practically had to prowl through the nightclubs in the city for a week before he felt nourished enough to not feel like he was going to collapse right where he stood.

"Wow," Joy breathed.

Malachi's wings flared without his control, preening. He cleared his throat, forcing them back to his sides.

Joy grinned, giving him a knowing look. She reached for his hand, tangling their fingers together again. Malachi squeezed her hand, fighting back the riotous swell of emotions under his breast.

"All right, then, demon boy. I'm ready for the grand tour."

Malachi smiled back at her. "As you wish, little tiger."

Seeing his house—Malachi refused to call it a castle— through Joy's eyes felt like nothing else. He'd sort of blended a mixture of old and new with the design of the interior. His heart thumped with excitement when he led her to the library, and he delighted in her happy little squeal as she rushed inside. God, the smell of her right now. He wanted it all over his abode, in every nook and cranny.

"How were you able to buy all these books?" she asked incredulously. Then she glanced up at him, looking sly. "Or did you "borrow" them? Emphasis on the borrow."

He grinned, flashing a hint of fang. "I did borrow them. In a sense."

Joy raised an eyebrow, her lips twitching. "Explain."

"I visited a few bookstores and used the aether to ... well, copy the essence of the books."

"That's a neat little trick, I have to admit," she said with a laugh. "If only." She trailed her fingers over the books on the shelves, her eyes greedily taking in the lettering on the spines. "Wow, your taste is, uh, very vast."

He'd taken everything—from fiction to nonfiction, from cookbooks to books on geography—greedy to know everything that concerned what was going to be his new home.

He grinned at her gobsmacked expression, at how she was slowly coming to realise there was no rhyme or reason to his collection; he'd simply put them on the shelf in the order he'd read—or wanted to read—them. "You should see my film collection."

Joy spun to stare at him. "Take me there. Now."

Malachi managed a soft laugh. His film room was almost exactly like his library, size-wise. Joy seemed even more excited in this room, darting from shelf to shelf.

"You have all seasons of *Total Drama Island*! And *Adventure Time*! And the *Regular Show*! Ah!"

Malachi had to bite the inside of his cheek. Holy shit she was so fucking cute he couldn't stand it.

"I can give you copies of anything you want," he offered carelessly. As long as he remained in the mortal realm, the magic forming them should hold.

Joy turned to stare at him. She looked like he'd just popped her brain like a grape. He moved closer to her, wanting—*needing* to touch her.

He cupped her throat and her jaw, his thumb stroking her cheek.

"That's too much," she breathed, swaying into his touch. "Surely that's too much?"

"Nothing's too much," he whispered. *Not for you*, he added silently.

She seemed to hear the words anyway, her scent going molten and sweet. Malachi leaned down to kiss her. She made a soft sound as their lips connected, and he felt that sound all the way down to his marrows. His wings spread, enveloping them against the shelf they were pressed against.

"I'm serious," she said after a few moments, panting into his mouth. Her hands were around his neck, and she was standing on the tips of her toes. She looked up, her doe, brown eyes meeting his. "I will literally make a list, Malachi. Don't tempt me."

He kissed her forehead, then her nose. Her lips spread into a smile she seemed to want to suppress, her scent going all buttery warm.

"I'm tempting you," he murmured.

Joy yanked him down to kiss him again, hungrily, desperately. Then she abruptly pulled away. He tucked his wings to his back to give her room to move as she meticulously did as she'd threatened, starting from one end of the room.

"I'm curious," she said, eyes darting in his direction as she perused the shelves. "Have you really watched everything in here?"

"I have not."

"Damn. That's disappointing."

Malachi's lips twitched. "Sorry to disappoint."

"How about the books? Read all of them?"

"I'm going to have to disappoint you again."

Joy laughed. "What's your favourite movie, then? Of the ones you've watched."

Malachi took a moment to think, rifling mentally through his watched shelf. He loved a good romantic movie; he loved action films—he had quite a vast taste, actually. But he seemed to lean more toward animated movies.

"*The Iron Giant*," he finally said. He loved that movie because it told the story of an outsider who simply wanted a home—wanted to belong. It was a story that said who you were didn't have to have anything to do with what you were born to do; you choose who you are. "I find the story very relatable."

Joy softened all over. Her eyes were shining. "I knew you had taste." Malachi's feathers rustled as he forced his wings to keep from spreading, though he couldn't quite prevent the soft smile from stretching his lips. "I'm sure you already know this considering how much time you've spent with me, but I love cartoons. Animated movies. All that. I love them with all my heart. *The Iron Giant* is an underrated gem and I'm glad you know how to appreciate art when you see it."

Malachi chuckled. "Animation is my favourite medium as well."

"I could tell." She winked. "How about books? Do you have a favourite?" Joy had finally reached the end of the shelf, and was beside the floor-to-ceiling windows, casually glancing outside. She let out a happy gasp. "Wait, you have a garden!"

"I do," Malachi said.

Joy turned to face him, her question and her current task forgotten. "Take me to your garden," she demanded.

Fuck. Was Malachi falling in love? Was this what it felt like? Every time she looked at him, it felt like all his organs were taking a tumble; like someone was squeezing his heart at the same time that the organ was inflating like an air balloon behind his ribs.

Rather than use the aether, Malachi took her hand, leading her out of the room, back down the stairs, past the kitchens, and out the back door.

Joy's sharp, wonderous inhale sent Malachi's chest puffing, his wings flaring before he could control them.

"Wow," Joy breathed.

The exit from the kitchen held three pathways, two that wrapped around the house on each side, and one leading straight ahead, right into the garden. All three pathways were bracketed by thick, tall hedges that were a deep green in the darkness.

The path to the garden spilled into a little conservatory, surrounded by hedges on all sides with more pathways leading deeper into the garden. This roofed little space had a small, stone fountain in the middle, with curved benches along the hedges on either side.

Bright flowers bloomed in the greenery of the conservatory. Malachi couldn't help but show off a little, his eyes flaring as he pulled from the aether.

The flowers began to change colour, flashing dully in the moonlight.

Joy glanced at him from over her shoulder, her lips curled into a happy smirk. "Show off," she teased, and Malachi's heartbeat did something complicated. "This is ... wow." She moved to the bench on the right side of the fountain and sank into it, staring around at the conservatory, then up through the glass ceiling at the house behind them. Malachi sat next to her, spreading his wing and draping it around her when she shifted closer to his warmth, which made his heart do that complicated thing again.

Joy shook her head, disbelieving. One of her hands had found their way into his feathers, and he tried not to shiver as she distractedly played with them.

"This place is actually ridiculous." Her voice softened, and she couldn't quite meet his eyes. "To be honest, I don't know how you stand it. It's ... it's a little big, isn't it? For you alone." Then she laughed, though it sounded strained. "I mean, unless you aren't alone! Maybe you have—I don't know. Friends. Partners. Lovers. People who visit."

"I don't," Malachi said. She looked sideways at him. "I don't," he repeated. "Have any of that," he clarified. He had to swallow past a sudden embarrassed lump in his throat, looking away, feeling a blush heat his cheeks. It was her scent, his need for her happiness and her vulnerability that had him admitting, "I thought a castle was romantic."

There. Her scent bloomed like a flower in the night, rarely seen and all the more intoxicating for it.

"Malachi," she whispered, "that's so sweet."

"I am not sweet."

She laughed, her scent brightening, warming further. "How long have you been in the mortal realm, by the way? Or do demons just come and go as they please?"

"I have been here for nearly two years," Malachi admitted.

"Only? But you've been here before, right?"

Malachi shook his head. "I have not. To answer your earlier question, while demons—or nicquiris, like myself—can travel to and fro through the Veil, we are not meant to remain in the mortal realm. However, we *can* remain by one of two ways; using a contract to a human as a tether, or acquiring a human soul."

"Ah." Joy nodded in understanding. "So, if someone sells their soul to you, you can stay here for as long as you want?"

"That is correct."

"It's kind of like the Underworld, eh?" Joy said, nudging her shoulder against his side. "You eat of the fruit of the place and now you can never leave, or something like that."

Malachi's lip twitched. "Something like that."

"Have you ever been back to hell, then? Gosh, it feels so weird referring to your home as that. No offence."

Malachi's eyes darkened. "Hell is not my home," he said roughly. "And I have not been back there since I left, nor do I intend to ever go back." He cleared his throat, trying to lighten the mood. "Why would I be offended? What else would you call it?"

"I don't know." Joy ducked her head. Her fingers were still tangled in his feathers, combing through the thick, fluffy strands. Malachi had his hands fisted in his lap. Her touch felt impossibly good. "Do demons not have families, then? There's no one you left behind in hell?"

Malachi paused. "I have ... memories of another ... one who was created at the same time as I was, but we were separated not long after our birth."

"Oh." Joy's scent mellowed. "I'm sorry."

Malachi wanted to shrug her off, to say it was fine, that he never knew them at all, but it wasn't really fine. He would've liked to know them. They'd probably been a nicquiri like he was. Had the Priest gotten to them? Were they, right now, trapped in hell, bound by the Priest's spells to make endless trips to and from the mortal realm, farming souls and emotions for the sect, while they slowly starved and wasted away?

The thought was too much to bear. Once upon a time, Malachi had dreamed of going back to free the rest of the auxiliaries, but his sect was one of—if not *the* largest sect in hell. There would've been hundreds of thousands of them; he never would have been able to do it, at least not alone. It made his heart break, so he forced himself not to think too much about it.

"What about you?" Malachi forced himself to ask. "Any family?"

Joy huffed out a breath. "Well, there's my aunt, who you know about. My parents died nearly three years ago now. Plane crash."

It was Malachi's turn to say, "I'm sorry," his wing tightening around her.

"Thank you." She burrowed into it like it was a blanket. "As for my other family, I have my best friend, who is practically my sister, Iyore, along with her fiancé, Malcom—though I see Malcom more as hers than mine. And that's about it." She dropped her hands to the bench, staring up through the glass ceiling at the glittery night sky, and the swollen, full moon.

She turned when she'd gotten her fill, and peered at Malachi from underneath her lashes.

Malachi was hit suddenly by the force of her beauty. The glow of the moonlight, along with the slowly morphing colours of the flowers around them turned her into a living, breathing painting. She looked like something ethereal—like a Sovereign—like if he reached out to try and touch her, she'd disappear, burst into a shower of sparks.

"You said hell isn't your home," she whispered, her long eyelashes fluttering each time she blinked. Malachi found himself mesmerised by the movement of them. "Can you tell me why not?"

Malachi forced himself to look away. "I was born to bring souls and emotions back to hell; I was a soldier, nothing more."

Joy's eyes felt heavy on the side of his face, her scent warm like sunlight.

"I'd like to think you're a little more than that, Malachi," she murmured sweetly, teasingly, the whispered words forcing him to look at her.

She smiled at him, and Malachi was utterly destroyed.

"I like to think so, too," he whispered.

At that moment, Malachi knew it like he knew his True Name. There would never be another. Joy was *it*. Could he let her go now? When there was so much to discover between them?

"Thank you for the food earlier, by the way," Joy whispered. "I forgot to say."

"You're welcome."

They stared at each other, something almost terrifying expanding in the air between them.

Malachi reached for the words building up in his throat, but they refused to form, that damnable fear holding him back.

Too much, too soon.

Joy abruptly stood. Her scent had changed, turned static with electricity, her body jittery as well. Her eyes were hard with determination.

"Malachi," she whispered, "take me to your bedroom."

Malachi stood as well. He extended his hand, trembling slightly when she tangled her fingers with his. Once again, he opted not to use the aether, leading her back into the house from the kitchens.

As he led her upstairs, from room to room, parlour to parlour, he could easily imagine her filling the space, with her bright scent and even brighter laughter.

Dangerous, Malachi, the voice of reason tried to warn.

He ignored it.

Joy stepped into his private chambers with wide, eager eyes.

His massive bed sat to the left from the door. It had a canopy, the gauzy cream curtains currently drawn, tied to the posts. The sheets were cream and red velvet, with a multitude of pillows. In the far right corner was an actual sunken tub, one of the more "modern" designs of the house. Magic had made that one possible; if he was going to be alone for the rest of his life, Malachi wanted to be alone in comfort.

Joy immediately raced to his bed, flying on top of it and bouncing slightly.

"Ah." She sighed, dropping onto her back, spreading her arms wide. "The sheets are so *soft*." She sat up. Her eyes twinkled. Malachi's heartbeat sped up.

She rubbed her thighs slightly together, her eyes growing dark, eyelids growing heavy. Malachi's blood responded, heating up in his veins.

She stared at him from lowered lashes for a moment, her scent doing something complicated. She smelled eager, aroused, but strangely melancholic at the same time.

Malachi's racing heart began to race for a different reason. Why did that look—that scent, despite its underlying heat—feel like a goodbye? His chest twisted painfully at the thought.

Joy stood. Malachi's heart pounded harder. With fear or anticipation, he wasn't sure

He blinked when she reached for the hem of her shirt, then smoothly pulled it off her frame. Her hands dropped to the elastic waistband of her joggers. She pushed them down to mid-thigh, then gave her hips a little wiggle to encourage them to pool at her feet, before she stepped out of them. He wanted to see her make that little wiggle again. She'd been wearing crocs, which she'd kicked off.

Now she stood in just her underwear, a soft pink lacy cotton that made her dark brown skin look lush and inviting.

"Come here," she said huskily, with a single crook of her finger.

Malachi obeyed, his body moving almost without his conscious permission, like he was hooked to strings and she was his puppeteer.

His wings flared wide when she looked up at him with those sultry eyes, his tail flicking with eagerness, his dick already stiff and ready.

"Take this off," she commanded, threading a finger through his smoky robes.

The robe slipped off his shoulders, melting into smoke and disappearing completely before they'd touched the ground. Joy released a soft puff of air, her eyes trailing all over his form.

"You're so beautiful," she whispered.

Malachi didn't know why he suddenly felt choked up. "I could say the same about you."

Joy smiled. She stood on the tips of her toes, closing her eyes and lifting her face in invitation, her lips pursed.

Without her watching, Malachi used the opportunity to greedily take in every inch of her form. Her round rosy cheeks, her thick lashes and full lips, all that gorgeous, deep brown skin; every dip and curve of her sexy, fat frame.

He had to stop his perusal too soon—not enough—because it felt like he could look at her for the rest of eternity, and they didn't have that much time. Instead of focusing on that, he slid his hands to her backside, enjoying her soft little exhale.

He lifted her up, off her feet, pressing her against his chest. She obligingly wrapped her legs around him as he finally captured her lips with his, swallowing her sweet, little sigh.

If this was to be the last time, then he was going to make sure it was one she never forgot.

TWELVE

Joy could feel it like a clock ticking in the back of her mind; their time was running out. This night wouldn't last forever; eventually, Malachi would have to go back to the scene and clear it up before the body was found, which meant he had to leave before sunrise. Once he fulfilled his end of the bargain, there would be nothing tying them together anymore.

At least, not unless—

Joy squashed the thought as fast as it appeared. There was no "unless". She had a life to get back to. New friends. Her family. All the plans she'd had to shove aside while she'd enacted her vengeance.

She didn't know if there was space for Malachi within all that. She hadn't *planned* for a space for Malachi within all that. She didn't even want to consider it, because even *thinking* about considering it made her feel like she was losing control. No, it made her feel like control was being *taken* from her, even though she knew it wasn't the fucking same.

She pressed herself harder against Malachi, wrapping her arms tightly around his neck. She moaned as he kissed her, deeply and passionately, exploring her mouth with a slow, deliberate intent, like he was content to do so forever. His dexterous tongue seemed to touch every inch of the cavern of her mouth, before thrusting deep into her throat, making her groan, her pussy gushing.

He only pulled away when she needed to breathe, her panting breaths puffing into his face.

His eyes burned like a brilliant red flame in the darkness. "How do you want me?" he whispered huskily.

Joy's cunt clenched. She'd never been the dominant one in the bedroom, happy enough to do whatever her partner wanted. But with Malachi ...

Maybe the incident had rewired her brain. Maybe she'd always been like this, but had never met someone to bring it out of her.

Or maybe it was just Malachi.

She rested her hands on his chest, shifting her legs. He took the hint, helping her slide down his hard body. She forced herself to take a step back, swallowing thickly.

"On the bed," she said.

He moved to the bed, adjusting until he was lying on his back on it, his head propped up slightly by the pillows. It was so fucking hot, how easily he did what he was told.

Joy took her bra off, letting it fall to the floor, then slid her panties down her hips.

"Fuck," he snarled, staring between her legs. She was so wet a thin string of her arousal connected in a line from her cunt to the seat of her panties, the sight of it erotic and unbearably lewd.

The panties slid down enough that the string disconnected. She stepped out of the cotton lace and watched as she literally dripped onto the hardwood floors, her pussy clenching hard at the sight.

"Fuck," Malachi said again, his hips churning, dick straining between his legs.

Joy couldn't help but slide her pointer and middle finger between her thighs, moaning as she stroked her swollen clit, her hands gliding easily through all that fucking wetness. She dipped her fingers into her hungry cunt, then slipped them back out to rub her clit again. Malachi watched her with hungry red eyes.

Slowly, Joy lifted her glistening fingers, showing him, before sliding them into her mouth.

"*Fuck*," Malachi snarled for the third time, his hips jerking abortively into the air.

Joy sucked her fingers clean. Then, panting, she crawled on top of him, stopping when she was straddling his thighs. His dick flexed as she watched, a pearl of pre-come beading at the head. She'd planned to take him into her mouth, but she couldn't help but inch forward until she was straddling his hips, her cunt poised over his dick, which lay flat against his belly.

She lowered her hips torturously slowly, biting her lower lip hard when her puffy pussy lips connected with his heated flesh, eagerly parting along the girth of his stiff length. By the time she was settled completely on top of him, they were both shaking with want. She rolled her hips, whimpering as those ridges around the base of his cockhead glanced over her throbbing, swollen, oversensitive clit.

"Oh God," she gasped.

Malachi groaned, hips twitching. He was fisting the sheets, not touching her, like he was waiting for permission.

"Good boy," Joy whispered.

Malachi's hips twitched again, his red eyes glowing.

Joy wanted to worship him. She wanted to fucking *mark* him like he'd subconsciously marked her, so he remembered her for the rest of his immortal life.

She began by kissing him—his lips, his forehead, his cheeks, his jaw. She trailed soft, open-mouthed kisses down his throat, along his collar bones.

By the time she made it to one of his nipples, he was shaking. She swirled her tongue around the peak, then sucked it into her mouth. Malachi gasped sharply, arching underneath her. Her fingers found his other nipple, squeezing and plucking with her thumb and pointer finger.

"Fuck, fuck—*Joy*."

She shifted to the other nipple to shower it with the same love with her mouth, enjoying the way he trembled and gasped her name in-between snarls and curses.

Then she trailed lower, across his firm stomach, down between his legs to his weeping dick.

He was panting like he'd just run a marathon. She looked up, meeting his eyes, his plum cheeks flushed so dark they looked almost black.

She curled a hand around his girth, stroking experimentally. She heard a rip, pleasure burning hot in her lower belly when she realised he was tearing at the sheets, all because she hadn't given him permission to touch her—to move.

Fuck. She pressed her slick thighs together, whimpering at the pressure around her clit.

She kissed the tip of his dick, eyes widening when she flicked her tongue out to taste.

"Delicious," she whispered. She could taste a bit of herself in the mix, which was erotic as fuck.

"Joy." Malachi sounded tortured.

She used her left hand to stroke his dick, while the other

went down, rolling his balls in her palm briefly before sliding even lower, between his cheeks.

"Okay?" she whispered, her heart rabbiting in her chest, her clit throbbing.

He lifted his legs in answer, balancing his feet on the bed.

"Good boy," she murmured.

He groaned as she took just the head into her mouth, sucking and flicking her tongue against the weeping slit at the same time that she pressed a finger against his rim.

Malachi's dick jerked hard in her mouth. "Fuck, stop— *stop*—I'm going to come," he cried.

Joy groaned, pulling off his dick with a lewd slurp. "Already?" she teased, feeling so high on the power she could fly with it.

"Please. *Please*."

And Joy couldn't wait any longer. She needed him inside her right fucking now. She moved abruptly, crawling up the length of his body until she was straddling his face. Malachi made a desperate, frantic noise, his eyes honed in on her pussy above him.

"Make me come," Joy demanded desperately.

"Yes," Malachi said, his hands coming up to hold her thighs.

"No." Joy gave them a gentle push, waiting until Malachi was fisting the sheets again. "No hands," she said roughly, locking her eyes with his.

His body jerked slightly. "Almighty. Fuck. Okay."

Joy gripped his horns for balance. "Okay? That doesn't hurt?"

"No," he rasped. "Please."

Fuck. She sank down onto his waiting mouth. He parted his lips eagerly, his tongue immediately sliding inside her.

"Fuck, *yes*." Joy shook uncontrollably when he slid his tongue back out, and the forked end found her clit and began to swirl rapidly around it. "Yes," she sobbed, helplessly rocking her hips into it, grinding onto his face. "Yes, Malachi. Please."

He lifted his head slightly, and his tongue suddenly went into a frenzy, lashing at her clit—fucking *vibrating* against it—until she was screaming her pleasure and gushing all over his face. From the corner of her eye, she saw his hips lift off the mattress, a tortured sound echoing in the back of his throat.

Joy didn't let herself even catch her breath, not wanting to tighten up again. She slid down his body on shaking legs, keeping her eyes on his as she balanced her left hand on his chest, and reached between her legs for his dick. She stroked the tips of her fingers over the slick, tapered head, before angling it at the entrance to her cunt.

She sank back, already out of her mind with it when only the tip pierced her. Her belly quivered, hungry for the almost-painful stretch of him filling her up, moving inside her.

"You can touch me," she gasped.

His hands went to her hips. "Thank you," he breathed, his red eyes glittering, knowing exactly what those words did to her.

"Fuck." She moved up a little, then sank again. Her eyes wanted to close with pleasure and concentration, but she didn't want to look away from him.

She lifted her hips once more, and sank again. She was sure she'd never been this wet in her life—could feel herself growing impossibly wetter at the slow, sinful stretch, her cunt hot and hungry for him completely filling her.

She kept up the pace, biting her lower lip, rolling her hips forward and then back, managing to take more and more of him with each aborted thrust of her hips.

Malachi didn't move, simply gripping her hips, letting her set the pace, which set her on fire like nothing else.

Tears spilled down her cheeks when he was finally fully inside her.

"Oh my God," she said, her thighs shaking. She felt like she could feel him in her throat. "Oh my God."

Malachi was biting his lower lip, eyes hooded, his hands digging so hard into her flesh she knew she'd have bruises. *Good*.

She balanced both her hands on his chest and began to move, her cunt gliding so easily along his length that Malachi's eyes rolled back. His mouth fell open, and she could see the physical strain in his muscles, in his clenched, trembling thighs as he fought the urge to thrust into her.

It filled her with indescribable power. She leaned back a little, cupping her tits and pinching her nipples as she rocked even slower, dragging a tortured growl from his throat, his head falling back into the pillows, his wings flaring wide on the mattress underneath him.

Eventually, even that slow ride was torture for her, and she began to speed up. She had to close her eyes now, nearly drooling as she rolled her hips back and forth, angling herself so his dick was grinding over the sensitive spot inside her. Stars burst behind her eyelids, and pleasure like nothing she'd ever felt overcame her senses.

"Fuck, my sweet, murderous Joy." Malachi sounded frantic. "Let me make you come."

Joy's pussy clenched eagerly.

"Ask nicely," she panted.

"Please," Malachi said immediately. "Please, let me make you come."

It was like a hair trigger. Joy's pussy seized up. She stiffened, squeezing her tits, sobbing as she spasmed around him so hard he was forced out of her while she squirted all over his hips and thighs.

"Fuck, fuck, Malachi," she sobbed, dropping her hands

onto his chest, her thighs quaking, pussy spasming.

"*Joy*." Malachi was arching underneath her, his dick jerking and weeping, his expression twisted into one of pleasurable agony, like her orgasm was his own.

She'd barely come down from it when she grabbed his length and angled it against her cunt, once again sinking down. The glide of it was so easy it was practically sinful, her cunt stretched to fit him like a glove.

Malachi let out a strangled shout and snapped his hips up. He squeezed desperately at her hips. "Fuck, sorry. *Sorry*."

Heat flooded her. "You *can*—Malachi—*fuck* me—you can fuck me—"

"Al-fucking-mighty." He adjusted his grip, digging his heels into the mattress. He lifted her slightly so she had more balance on her knees, then he began to fuck her.

Joy's nails dug into his chest as she took his frantic pounding with harsh cries, his hips slapping wildly into the backs of her thighs.

"Yes," she cried. "Fuck. Jesus bloody fucking Christ. Yes, yes, yes, yes—"

His thrusts soon turned sloppy, uncoordinated, and he slid his tail between their bodies to her clit. A few rough strokes against her swollen flesh and she was gone.

He grunted and abruptly stopped moving, holding her down so she was forced to come on his dick, gushing and clenching all over him, while she was sure she could feel her brain leaking out of her ears.

"Tell me I can come," Malachi rasped urgently, voice thick. "I'm—can I—please, Joy, can I—?"

Joy had barely gasped out, "yes," when he roughly snapped his hips up once, twice, stiffening with a bitten-off shout as he finally came, rutting and pumping his load into her. Feeling him spasming inside her—filling her up— seemed to drag her orgasm out, until she felt like she would pass out from the intensity.

She collapsed onto his chest when she was back to earth, feeling like she'd been turned completely inside out.

Malachi didn't think he was in this plane of reality anymore. Surely his soul had left his body and was drifting above the heavens? Joy lay limp and heavy on his chest, her breaths and heartbeat calming slowly.

Her suspicious little sniff brought him crashing back down to earth. He gathered her close, wincing as his soft dick slipped out of her.

"Hey, hey, what's wrong?" he asked urgently, nosing at her cheek, though he couldn't really smell any sadness, just her pleasure and happiness.

"It's nothing—I'm just. I just realised I'm so fucking happy," she confessed, tilting her face to stare up at him. He hated the tears that filled her eyes, but he loved the way she smelled right now. He slid his thumbs along the bottom of her lower lids, wiping them away. "It just hit me again that he's really gone. I had a crush on him, you know?" For a brief moment, Malachi saw absolute red. "I thought—I had a plan—I was going to make friends, and I thought about dating, and he was so nice and funny at work—" She cut herself off, sniffing. Malachi's hand was cupping her cheek. He remained silent, letting her collect herself. "It felt worse in the aftermath, like—how could I have ever—? And how could I tell anyone? He'd just—I knew he would—"

"Joy," Malachi began.

"I know, I know. It took me some time, but I know. I didn't do anything wrong. *He* did. But now he's fucking *dead*. God, I-I feel so fucking relieved." She laughed, the sound maniacal. "Does that make me a bad person?"

"The worst," Malachi said solemnly, his heart soaring when she laughed.

He pressed kisses to her soft lips, over and over until she stopped crying, exhaling shakily into his mouth. Malachi held her, simply held her, while the rest of his world felt like it was falling apart, at the same time that something in his chest was fitting into place, a missing puzzle piece finally found.

"Joy," he whispered after a few moments.

"Yes?" she replied sleepily.

That ache Malachi was beginning to grow familiar with burned sweetly behind his ribs. "Are you comfortable?"

"Yes." She sighed, soft and sweet.

Malachi adjusted his position, hugging his arms around her. He waved a hand to get rid of any stains and fluids, then tucked the sheets, warm and clean, around them. He wished he could spend the rest of eternity sheltered like this in her warm embrace. When he turned his head to look down at her, he could see that her eyes were closed, and she was clearly seconds from falling asleep, though she was trying to fight it.

Lips twitching, feeling so fucking fond, Malachi whispered, "Joy."

"Yes?"

His lips stretched wider, into a soft grin. "Go to sleep."

She frowned, like she wanted to argue, but then she let out the tiniest little exhale.

And finally, for what Malachi assumed must've been the first time in a long time, Joy slept.

THIRTEEN

Malachi didn't want to move. Joy was so deeply asleep she was snoring a little, drooling onto his chest. Panic made Malachi's breaths come fast, though he forced his body to remain relaxed, not wanting to disturb her.

In a few hours, the sun would come up. Malachi had to deal with the body before then; he couldn't risk it staying any longer. The longer he left it off, the more it was likely to be discovered before he finished his end of the bargain.

And once he did ... then what?

Could he leave Joy here, in his bed, in his house—could he come back to her? What if she noticed he was gone, put two and two together, and decided she didn't want anything more?

Malachi wanted her. He wanted her like he'd never wanted anything in his life before.

He moved, something bright but painful tightening

around his chest when Joy's expression twisted with irritation at the disturbance.

"Sorry," he murmured, his lips twitching. "Joy."

She frowned, her lips forming a pout.

Malachi bit his lip. "Joy," he repeated.

"What?" she complained.

Malachi had to swallow to wet his suddenly dry throat. "I'm—I'm leaving. I'm going to—to clean up the crime scene, so to speak."

Joy stilled, processing his words. He heard her heartbeat go haywire, her scent as well. His arms tightened slightly around her, hope filling his chest like a slowly swelling balloon.

Then Joy turned away from him abruptly, her heart still skittering like a rabbit's underneath her ribs. "Yeah. Okay. You do that."

Malachi didn't move, his arms limp around her. His chest abruptly deflated. Should he ask? But how could he, when he didn't know *what* to ask? How to express what he wanted? He couldn't just tell her he wanted to spend the rest of his life with her; humans seemed to need more time to think about such things; it would send her running for the hills if he expressed how certain he was.

Too much, too soon.

But he had to at least try.

"Joy," he began, his voice a low whisper.

"Don't," she said, a little sharply. He heard her swallow. "Don't," she repeated, softer. "*Please.*"

Malachi tried to breathe normally. After a few moments, he had to ask—he had to *know*.

"Can you at least tell me why?"

Joy was silent. He was almost afraid she wouldn't say anything when she finally turned around to face him again. Her eyes were shiny.

"I just—it's too much." Malachi's heart shrivelled to a dried up husk. "I just feel I need some time, after everything, to learn to be on my own again. I can't—it feels like ... there was my grief, then my work ... and then *him*; then there was— for a long time, there was just *nothing*—not even me." She blinked rapidly, fighting back tears. "Then there was my revenge. And then ... there was you." Her gaze dropped to the sheets. "All with absolutely no space in between. It's just ... it's too much. I need to be on my own for a while. I need some time so I can find *me* again." She met his eyes again, her doe brown eyes shiny. "Do you understand?"

"Yes," Malachi whispered, even though his heart was fucking breaking. He cupped her face, wiping away the tears gathering like dewdrops on her eyelashes. "I understand."

She pressed into his touch, her eyes clenched shut, her jaw gritted.

I can wait, he wanted to tell her, urgently, desperately. *I'll wait for you. For however long it takes.*

But he didn't think it would be fair to ask. He held her instead, waiting, listening to her breaths, until her body softened and her breathing deepened into the rhythm of sleep.

He retracted his arms from around her and slid out of the bed. She immediately pulled the covers around her, like she subconsciously felt naked and she wanted to hide.

Malachi moved through the aether to the crime scene, unable to be in her presence any longer. His chest felt like it was caving in. Fuck, he wasn't going to be able to go back to that room ever again. Would he be able to go back to his house? With her scent, her laughter—the memories of her holding his hand—of her making love to him in his bed—

He shook his head violently. He couldn't bear to think about it right now.

Despite the fear taking root deep in his stomach—once

the bond dissolved, and he lost his contract with Joy, would Desmond's soul be enough to carry him until he found another one?—he manipulated the aether to clean up the room, getting rid of all the angry stains of red, along with any signs anyone else had been here. The man's body was next, the stab wounds closing up with a mere thought from Malachi.

When he was done, the man lay prone on his bed on his back, sheets tucked around him, one hand on his pillow, the other on his chest, like he'd simply died in his sleep.

The bond in his chest snapped the moment he'd finished, making him gasp. He'd gotten used to the warmth, the tether linking him to Joy, and felt bereft now that it was gone.

He straightened, hands clenching by his sides, bracing himself for the loss of power. While he did feel weaker, he must've underestimated the power of the soul he'd acquired; he didn't feel as weak as he'd expected, and he wasn't flickering between the mortal and astral realms like he'd feared.

But he was still afraid to trust it. For now, Malachi had one last spell he needed to do, then he was going to conserve his energy until he could find another contract, and hopefully, another soul. Just to be safe.

After, he would have to learn to go back to a life where Joy had never existed.

Joy hadn't meant to fall back to sleep. When she opened her eyes, waking up from what was probably the best sleep she'd had since the incident, surprisingly, she found herself back in her place, tucked into her own sheets. She sat up with a lurch, her heart pounding. For a delirious moment, she wondered if it had all been a dream.

The flat was empty. It felt ... weird. Not just empty, cavernous. Joy distractedly rubbed at her chest; she felt like there was a hole behind her ribs, like something was missing.

Guilt and a flash of pain stabbed her at the memory of Malachi's voice—of the naked hope in it when he'd said her name.

She clenched her eyes shut, violently shaking her head. It was over. He must've completed his end of the bargain, hence this emptiness in her chest.

She left her bed, startled when she found herself dressed in the clothes she'd worn to Malachi's castle. Her crocs were beside the rest of her shoes by the wall. He must've used his magic to get her here, so he wouldn't disturb her.

The pain came again. She ignored it. This was good. This was fine. What good would saying "goodbye, it was nice while it lasted" have done, anyway? It was better like this; ripping the BandAid off and all that.

Joy squared her shoulders. It was over; it was done. It was time for her to get back to her old life, starting off with renting a bigger flat. She hadn't lied to Malachi; she needed some time to be on her own—to *live* again, now that her rapist was dead and no longer had that strong of a hold on her and her life.

She was sure, the more she got back into the rhythm of how her life had been before the incident, whatever lingering feelings she felt for Malachi would begin to feel more and more alien, and like it'd never happened at all.

FOURTEEN
A few weeks later

Joy entered Argungu, clutching the strap of the purse slung over her shoulder. She looked around, then beamed when she spotted her best friend waving dramatically at her from one of the booths in the corner of the restaurant.

"Gosh, I feel like I haven't seen you in forever!" Iyore exclaimed as Joy approached their table, standing up so she could hug her.

Joy hugged her tightly, laughing. "I know. It's been a minute, abi?"

"There she is," Malcom, Iyore's fiancé, said, standing up as well. He was even taller than Iyore; they always joked that he could've been a basketballer if Nigeria took training their athletes more seriously. His skin was a dark umber, his head completely shaved bald, and a full beard surrounded his lips, jaw, and throat. "Wetin happen na, Joy? It's like you disappeared off the face of the earth."

Joy pretended to grimace, waving her hand flippantly, hugging him before sliding into the booth opposite them. She reached for one of the complimentary sachets of plantain chips laid out in a small woven basket in the middle of the table.

"Oh, you know," she said, ripping the packet open. "I just had some things I had to do." Iyore's expression was carefully neutral; she probably thought Joy had needed time off to get her mental health in order after ... everything, and she wasn't exactly wrong. Malcom remained blissfully unaware, munching on his own opened sachet of chips. "How about you two? Have you set a wedding date yet?" She leered.

It was Malcom's turn to be flippant, though, strangely, Iyore was blushing hotly, evident in the smile she was trying to suppress, her eyes downturned, lips pursed.

"We're taking our time," Malcom said, grinning lazily. "I can't wait to call this one my wife"—he jerked his thumb in Iyore's direction—"but I do like the ring of "fiancée". Figure I'd milk that out for as long as possible." He turned to waggle his eyebrows at the fiancée in question.

"Malcom," Iyore admonished with a giggle, pushing his shoulder playfully.

Malcom grinned, leaning over to smack a quick kiss onto her cheek. "You know I'm joking, yeah? I honestly can't wait to marry you."

Iyore blushed harder, meeting his eyes. "I know. Me too."

Joy felt so fucking warm—so full already, even though they hadn't yet eaten. She'd been afraid at first, when she'd first come back home and Iyore had invited her to meet Malcom; she'd thought she'd feel like a third wheel. But she never had. Malcom really was perfect for her best friend; there was no one better Joy would have chosen for her.

She noticed the waiter approaching their table with the

menus and beamed.

"Are we ready to order?"

An hour or two later, after a ton of laughter, the repetition of stories they'd shared over a million times but just never seemed to get tired of, Joy felt full in both her belly and her heart. The ever-persistent hole in her chest could almost be ignored. Almost.

She, Iyore, and Malcom exited the restaurant, then the mall itself.

"Do you want to go dancing?" Iyore said suddenly, her voice high with energy. "I don't know; it's been a while! I feel like dancing."

Malcom laughed, leaning over to kiss her. "You don't mind if I rain check, babe? I've got an early start tomorrow, and I'm honestly exhausted."

"Of course not," Iyore said, kissing him again. "You don't mind, do you, Joy?"

"Why are you asking me?"

Iyore smacked her in the arm, making them all laugh.

"You ladies take the car; I'll order a Bolt. Have fun, eh? But not *too* much fun." He winked, handing Iyore his keys.

Iyore giggled. They kissed again, then he left the parking lot in the direction of the street to order his Bolt. Iyore took Joy's hand, leading her where Malcom had parked his car.

She started it, then turned to smirk slyly at Joy. "So," she began, the engine rumbling between them.

Joy's heart began to beat strangely. "So ..." she said, raising a questioning eyebrow.

Iyore giggled. "Did you manage to meet someone since I last saw you? You're glowing!"

"What? No." Joy squirmed where she sat. "Of course not. I didn't meet anyone. Don't be ridiculous," she said, but to her horror, she began to blush.

"You're blushing!" Iyore practically screamed, making Joy wince.

"I'm not blushing," she said, blushing harder. Of course she was glowing; killing the man who'd raped you and fucking the sexy demon who helped you to get away with it would probably do that to a person.

The thought of Malachi brought a painful twinge to Joy's chest. Her hands clenched in her lap. Over the past few weeks as she'd rebuilt the life her victim had unwittingly destroyed, she'd felt lighter and happier as she'd put the pieces back together. She'd resumed her graphic design business; she'd gotten a better flat; she'd even visited Aunty Paloma to let her know the deed was done, valiantly ignoring her aunt's curious eyes when she said nothing more than that.

She'd managed to sign on a huge client last week, which had led her to making the decision to quit her day job; she didn't really need it, had only held onto it thanks to the lingering belief of her late father's that being an entrepreneur wasn't a "real" job.

Rather than try to get new friends, she'd decided to give Iyore's and Malcom's friends another try. She hadn't been able to avoid Malcom when she'd come back to Nigeria—he was a package deal with Iyore, obviously—but after her parents' deaths and she'd dug into her work to avoid her grief, Joy had cancelled and flaked on so many plans with their friends that Iyore had eventually been the only one left standing. She hadn't thought she could try with the others again.

But she had, of course, overblown the whole thing. These people wouldn't be friends with Iyore if they were horrible people, after all, and they'd perfectly understood. So, Joy guessed she had actual friends, now. Still new, still tentative, but feeling real with each and every day that passed.

She didn't care one bit how her rapist had been found, if Malachi had made it look like he'd simply disappeared, or if he'd let it look like he'd somehow been mauled by a bear in his sleep. Her life was officially back on track.

But that persistent ache in her chest lingered. No matter what she did, the hole simply refused to go away.

"Joy?" Iyore's voice registered. It sounded like this wasn't the first time she'd said her name. "You okay, babe?"

Joy snapped out of it, forcing a quick grin. "I'm fine. I'm good. Where are we going anyway? I'm really glad you suggested this because I really do feel like dancing." And she meant it. Perhaps she'd meet a nice, sexy stranger, and it'd help her forget.

She *needed* to forget.

Iyore let her change the subject, grinning sunnily. "Where else?" she asked playfully.

As usual, Sound Control was packed on a Thursday. It was strictly Afrobeats night, which was unsurprisingly their most popular night of the week. The dancefloor was already packed despite it being only ten o'clock, with a remix of one of Joeboy's songs blasting through the speakers.

Joy's heart lurched with an anxiety she couldn't manage to shake off when Iyore led them to the bar. Her eyes locked like a hawk on the vodka and coke she ordered, making sure no one slipped anything into her drink. Even when the bartender passed the drink to her, safe and sound, she still couldn't be sure.

The glass could've been stained—the bartender might've had quick fingers—someone could've done something—

A pulse of pure fury and anguish beat in her stomach, which she quickly suppressed. Funny enough, *he* hadn't even been the one to slip anything in her drink; he'd arrived late to the get together, and had been well across the room when Joy began to feel the effects. The way he'd pretended to be so concerned, when all along he'd just seen it as his opportunity.

Joy gritted her teeth, forcing herself to remember her blade sinking into his stomach, over and over, the warmth of his blood spilling across her knuckles, staining her red and white dress. Like it was therapy, she felt her heartbeat slow, her anxiety bleeding out of her limbs.

She glanced at her best friend, her soulmate—the one person on this earth she knew she could hundred percent trust, and bravely took a sip of her drink.

It felt like walking off a cliff. It felt like taking back something she hadn't even known she'd lost. Her hand was shaking slightly, and she still felt anxious as fuck, but Iyore was here. Iyore wouldn't let anything hurt her.

"Let's dance!" Iyore said with excitement, grabbing her arm.

They began to shout along to the music as they made their way to the dancefloor, their hips shimmying. Joy truly let go of her inhibitions, laughing as Iyore twisted around to grind on her, her best friend laughing as well.

Iyore turned around again, finishing her drink with a quick gulp, carelessly dropping the plastic cup on the dancefloor. She wrapped her arms around Joy's neck, leaning close to whisper into her ear.

"Don't look now, but that guy has been staring at you since we entered!"

Joy tried not to stiffen. Her stomach squirmed with a

mixture of discomfort and only a little bit of anticipation. Could she do this? Would she be able to stand the touch of another person—another *man*, at that?

You stood Malachi's touch fine.

That was different, she argued at her subconscious.

Malachi had felt like a dream, like something stolen; a brief pocket of time that had felt so real as it simultaneously felt like a fantasy.

The yawning ache in her chest forced Joy to straighten her shoulders. She couldn't keep living like this. Malachi was gone. Her throat thickened. She'd practically driven him away, and he wasn't coming back.

She wrapped her arms around Iyore's hips, forcing her lips to curve up into a careless smile. "Is he behind me?" she asked playfully.

"Yup!" Iyore said happily, unaware of Joy's brief turmoil. "He's by the wall, in the corner."

Joy slowly, casually turned her head, like she was simply perusing the dancing bodies around them.

And froze when her eyes alighted on familiar horns. Dark purple wings. Her eyes locked with the familiar bright red of Malachi's before she could stop herself, her stomach immediately bursting to life with what felt like a million butterflies.

Joy spun back around, her heart in her throat. No. What the fuck? No. She couldn't hear the music anymore; all she could hear was her heartbeat, pounding loudly in her eardrums. The butterflies swarming in her stomach made her feel slightly ill.

How come no one had noticed him? Was she the only one who could see him?

"Did you see him?" Iyore asked with excitement. "Tall, dark, and handsome? And I do mean that in the most literal sense of the phrase." She giggled. Could she not see him the way Joy saw him? Was it a trick of his? Or was Iyore referring to someone else? "He's wearing all black, and honestly, I didn't think I was attracted to guys with long hair, but I have to say, he is rocking the shit out of that afro." Iyore leered.

Despite herself, Joy burst out laughing. Long hair? It *had* to be him. She swallowed thickly.

"By the wall," she said just to confirm, her voice strangely high-pitched, "right in the corner?"

"That's the one." Iyore beamed.

Joy's heart leapt. Strangely, she felt shy. Nervous.

She turned to look again, but he was gone.

Disappointment sent her heart crashing down to her feet like lead. She turned back around, clenching her jaw, then relaxing it. She couldn't help but glance again, looking wildly around the club, but he was gone. Had she imagined him?

She shook her head. She wanted to lie to herself that it didn't matter, but she was so fucking tired of lying.

She missed him. So fucking much. The dry, formal way he spoke. How he'd held her hand while she'd panicked in the darkness, his glowing red eyes focused completely on hers. The way he had sex, so eagerly and intensely, letting her take all the control. That first time he'd laughed—his voice when he'd said he'd built himself a fucking castle because he thought it was romantic.

Fuck. She missed him, she missed him, she missed him.

But she didn't know what the fuck she was going to do about it. Sure, she'd managed to tape bits of her soul back together—she felt as close as she'd ever come to feeling whole since the incident—but she didn't know how she could reconcile the life she now had with a fucking demon.

It had to have been easy for Aunty Paloma, already cut off from the rest of the world; she must've had nothing to lose, living like a hermit so she could hide her demon partner, who Joy was going to meet officially during the Easter celebrations.

Then again, didn't Aunty Paloma say Klaus liked to go on walks? Surely, people saw them when they did? And Aunty Paloma was an artist; matter of fact, she'd invited Joy to one of her art shows in the summer. Which Klaus was supposedly going to attend.

Joy paused. So, maybe Aunty Paloma wasn't a hermit. She probably had friends Joy was unaware of. And she still had Klaus.

Malachi lived in the mortal realm, didn't he? He'd said hell wasn't his home. Not anymore.

Hope and possibility sprouted to life in Joy's chest.

Then it quickly shrivelled and died when she remembered their last night together—when he'd used his magic to send her back to her place; when she'd practically said goodbye.

"What are you doing for Easter, by the way?" Iyore asked abruptly.

Joy blinked herself back to the present. "I'm spending it with my aunt. Why?"

"Oh, that's great!" Iyore beamed. "How's that going?"

"Quite well, thank you." Joy had told her about recently reconnecting with her long-lost family. "What about you?"

Iyore suddenly looked nervous, her throat bobbing. "I told Malcom about ... about my uncle."

Everything in Joy turned to ice. Fuck. She'd forgotten about that bastard.

"The truth is, *I've* been the one putting off the wedding," Iyore admitted, a little shamefully. Joy tightened her embrace around her, wanting her to know she was supported. It worked, because Iyore straightened. "It was supposed to be Easter, originally, though it's too late for that now. It's just—I know—I just *know* it—once we set a date and get everything into motion, even if I don't give him an invitation, someone's going to bring him. He's my mother's brother; there's no way he won't attend. And I can't tell anyone why I don't want him to be there." Her lower lip wobbled.

"Oh, honey," Joy said, heart breaking as she pulled her close.

"We're supposed to be dancing," Iyore said, but she held Joy just as tightly.

For a moment, they just stood, swaying slightly to the music, letting the moving bodies of the crowd rock and shift them around the dancefloor, rather than fight the current and block anyone's path.

An idea lit up in Joy's head, making her heartbeat pound. She clutched at Iyore's back, swallowing with difficulty.

Once the idea took root, she couldn't shake it off. This was her best friend—Iyore's wedding—her *happiness*, she was talking about. It had nothing to do with Malachi.

But if this meant she could see her demon again, at least one more time, then Joy was going to grab the excuse with both arms open wide.

FIFTEEN

Malachi told himself one more day—one more day to
wallow around his house like a ghost haunting the halls, then
he'd go out and feed. He didn't realise how much magic he
was burning just to keep himself from starving and wasting
away in his isolation, until he'd literally passed out one night
and had woken up in hell.

At first, he thought he was having a vivid nightmare. He
was back in his concrete cell, lying on the elevated slab that
had once been his bed. Runes and sigils marked the walls and
the floors, alive with the magic of the Priest. The strange chill
of the room settled onto him—*into* him, digging into his
bones like a virus. This was real.

No, no, no—

He'd escaped. He'd thought he was free.

Fuck. He should've gone to feed earlier. The human
clubs were always overwhelming in their intensity, emotions

swirling thick like clouds around the dancefloor, but it was still better than nothing.

Malachi had just wanted to drown in his self-pity for a little longer, and look where that had gotten him.

Hunger, painful and familiar, clawed at his stomach, his veins turning cold with abject terror.

Like his fear had summoned him, he heard the clink of the Priest's many necklaces as the archdemon walked down the stone corridor to his prison. Every inch of him tensed automatically, the sound like a trigger. His wings drew tightly into his back, his tail curling around his hips, his eyes shaking where they had automatically trained down on grey concrete.

Get out of here! His mind urged. Magic still burned in his core—he could still feel the aether around him. It would take some effort, but he could leave—

His body refused to move.

The stone door slid quietly open at the Priest's command, and Malachi's system automatically shut down in defence.

The Priest approached, his bare feet quiet on the concrete, necklaces clinking. Malachi realised faintly he was shaking. His claws dug harshly into his palms, slicing into his flesh, his blood dripping down his fists onto the floor.

"Well," the Priest said, his voice sending Malachi's insides shrivelling like an earthworm sprinkled with salt. "I didn't think I'd ever see you here again."

The Priest stood at a towering ten feet, his great, curved black horns excluded.

"Where have you been all this time, hm?" the Priest continued, like they were having a lovely chat. "In the mortal realm, I assume? I have to say, of all the nicquiris that have escaped my control, you were the most shocking."

Malachi refused to respond. He grasped desperately at the

aether, gathering all the magic he had to get him out of here safely.

It felt like looking for a needle in a haystack. Like grasping at cobwebs for an anchor. The strain made his temples throb; the sigils on the walls must've still been active, fighting to prevent Malachi's escape.

"You must've thought I had sentries after you."

Malachi couldn't help but look up in shock. The Priest's expression morphed into one of delight at landing the blow, his lips twisted with faux pity.

"Please," he said, beginning to laugh. "How typical to think yourself so important." He towered over Malachi, leaning down slightly like he wanted his next words to sink in. "For every nicquiri I manage to lose, the Sovereign makes ten more. In the grand scheme of things, you are nothing."

Malachi finally had a grasp on the aether. He bit back a shout as he was sent practically hurtling through time and space, until he was back in his bed in his castle.

The room flickered around him as he stared, going from polished wooden floors to dusty, old concrete.

Malachi clenched his eyes shut, breathing in deep. He felt ashamed, but he headed to the west wing to his main bedroom.

He hadn't been here since Joy. Her scent had since faded, but when he climbed into the mattress and pressed his face to the sheets, he felt like he could still smell her on the pillows, even though they'd since been magically cleaned.

Malachi knew he had to make another contract, preferably one that lasted as long as Desmond's had. Ideally, he needed another soul. He needed both at the same time.

But for now, he just let himself breathe. He didn't know what was worse, that his sect had apparently not given a shit when he'd disappeared, or that he'd apparently *wanted* them to.

Malachi had forced himself to go to the club after that. He couldn't risk losing control again. He could never go back there, ever again. He'd barely settled to feed on the humans' swirling emotions when she'd appeared like a fucking mirage within the crowd.

Joy.

She was wearing a sexy little black leather skirt, with a colourful Ankara blouse with long puffy sleeves that exposed her midriff. Next to her was someone he didn't recognise, a tall, thin light-skinned woman with a shoulder-length afro left to flow down to her shoulders. She was dressed in tight white jeans, and a differently-patterned Ankara top, though hers was a tube that went around her chest—her stomach, shoulders, and arms left exposed.

Malachi watched, like a fucking creep, as they headed to the bar. They moved with the easy camaraderie of a long friendship, hands landing on hips, fingers on arms, as they subconsciously guided themselves to the bar to prevent bumping into anyone.

Malachi's eyes blazed, and he burned even more magic he couldn't afford to just so he could scent her over the crowd, hear her heartbeat.

He stiffened when he smelled the scent of anxiety as she watched the bartender make her drink. She held it in one hand when he was done, and Malachi could practically taste her panic.

He made to move forward, just as Joy glanced at the woman beside her. Her breaths slowed, as did her heartbeat, and she took a sip of her drink.

Malachi retreated. He should leave. Seeing her again was

more painful than he'd realised. He hadn't thought they'd bump into each other again, but how hadn't he? They lived in the same fucking city.

He would have to move, probably. He didn't think he'd survive seeing her again.

"Don't look now, but that guy has been staring at you since we entered!" the friend suddenly said.

Malachi puffed up with rage, possessiveness, and jealousy when he scented a hint of Joy's interest.

"Is he behind me?" Joy asked, sounding sly.

"Yup! He's by the wall, in the corner."

Malachi didn't know the friend was talking about him until Joy was already turning, her eyes landing right on his.

For a moment, time stood still.

Joy's eyes widened. She abruptly looked away, her heartbeat skittering underneath her ribcage.

Malachi didn't want to know what came next. Like a coward, he retreated into the aether, too afraid to watch as she put up her walls once more.

The castle was too big. Malachi paced in one of the smaller downstairs parlours. Once he secured himself a long contract, he was going to downsize it. Perhaps he really should consider moving.

Fuck. *Joy*. Fuck, fuck.

He wanted to see her again. Fuck, fuck, he missed her. His thoughts raced, desperately retracing over his steps on their last night together.

Had he fucked everything up by sending her off, taking the cowardly way out instead of saying goodbye to her face? Then again, he could take a hint. She'd wanted space, and

he'd given it to her. Saying goodbye would have just dragged out the inevitable.

He did wish he'd told her he'd wait for her after all, delicate human sensibilities be damned.

A few hours later, and it seemed the universe had heard his wish; Malachi felt a tug underneath his breastbone; he heard the whisper of his name.

He stilled. The noise from the cartoon he'd been unsuccessfully trying to distract himself with—they all made him think of Joy, whether or not he'd watched them with her —faded to the background.

He felt the tug again, and the whisper was louder this time, in a voice he recognised.

Heart in his throat, butterflies in his stomach, Malachi let himself be pulled.

SIXTEEN

Joy knelt in the middle of a circular rune drawn with white chalk, wearing nothing but a bathrobe. The space was new—it was a proper bedroom, with two windows and two doors, one leading presumably to the bathroom and the other to the rest of her house? Flat?

The moment he appeared, Joy stood.

Malachi felt like he couldn't breathe. She smelled like nerves. Like sweetness and arousal and determination and everything Malachi had ever wanted.

"I'm here to make a deal," she said, tilting her chin up, bravely meeting his eyes despite the hint of insecurity he could smell in her scent.

Malachi couldn't help it. His lips quirked. Joy's heartbeat skipped, her own lips twitching, her scent blooming with happiness. Fuck, Malachi had fucking missed her.

"That much is obvious," he recited, like they'd chosen to

do this on purpose. "You reek of bloodthirst," he continued, and to his surprise, she did, though her other emotions had slightly overshadowed it. Malachi smiled wider. Sweet, murderous Joy. He hoped she never fucking changed. "You have summoned me to kill someone for you."

Joy was practically vibrating where she stood, her hands clutching at the tie that kept her robe tightly shut. Her nipples were stiff, poking through the thin material of her robe. Malachi's dick began to stiffen.

"No," Joy said, slightly breathlessly. "*I* want to kill someone. I want *you* to make it look like an accident."

Malachi's tongue felt too heavy for his mouth when he said, "You haven't brought a sacrifice."

He watched, in what almost felt like slow motion, as Joy's robe dropped.

"I offer you my body." Fuck, fuck, fuck. Fucking Almighty.

"And what am I supposed to do with your body?"

"Anything you want."

"I accept," Malachi said roughly, desperately. "Say the vow."

Her voice was breathless as she recited, "Igris, entis, untis, represe."

Malachi didn't wait for the bond to settle over him before he was stalking across the circle, cupping the full globes of her ass in his palms and lifting her off the floor.

He swallowed her moan into his mouth, kissing her like he was a drowning man finally coming up for air. She kissed him just as hard, just as desperately, fisting his hair before trailing her hands all over his face and jaw, like she was trying to imprint the shape of him back onto her fingers.

Eventually, they had to pull apart to breathe.

"Joy," Malachi said, elated, disbelieving. "*Joy*."

"I've missed you," Joy said shyly, her scent so bright

Malachi almost felt drunk with it.

He had to kiss her again. She bit his lip, then sucked on his tongue when he slid it into her mouth. Malachi's body shook. Need burned in his gut, making his dick leak. He shoved his hands underneath her robe, groaning when they encountered bare flesh. He walked forward until they landed on the bed with him on top of her, then pressed his hand between her legs.

"Fucking Almighty," he rasped, his hips jolting into the mattress. She was so fucking *wet*.

"I'm ready," Joy gasped, arching into his touch. "I got myself ready—before I summoned you—"

"Almighty," Malachi groaned, his hips jolting again. Like he wanted to make sure, he used his magic to get rid of his claws and slid two fingers inside her, his mouth falling slack when they entered her effortlessly.

"Malachi," she cried, arching as he began to roughly fuck her with them, his thumb rubbing firm circles onto her clit.

She clawed at his arms, her thighs beginning to shake. "Oh my God, oh my God, oh my God," she whimpered.

She made a completely animal noise when she came, seizing up around his fingers, gushing all over his hand and the bed.

Malachi leaned up quickly, taking her lips in a brief kiss, grasping his leaking dick and aiming it at her greedy little cunt.

"Yes, yes, yes." She sobbed, spreading her thighs wider for him, lifting her hips.

He went slow, but still sank in easily, easier than he'd had the previous times. She must've used a toy; she must've been at it for some time—stretching herself for his dick, dripping onto the summoning circle as she'd called him.

Malachi helplessly slammed the rest of his length into her. Joy's eyes rolled back, her cunt clamping around him.

Malachi grunted and had to stop, literally fucking whining as she came around him, her pussy like a vice.

She melted into the bed when it was over, her body shaking.

"Holy shit," she panted, still trembling. "I never used to care about size, you know? You've completely ruined me."

"Good," Malachi said darkly.

"Don't stop," she whispered. "Fuck me, Malachi. Show me who your dick belongs to."

"Fuck," he cursed, and began to do as he was told, his hips slapping into hers.

"Fuck," Joy cried. "*Yes.*"

Using his wings for leverage, Malachi leaned up so he was balanced on his knees, his hands gripping her hips. He lifted her slightly off the mattress so she was balanced on her upper back, tilting her hips up for a better angle, then resumed his strokes.

Joy was reduced to drooling and babbling, her hands fisting the sheets on either side of her. Her tits bounced with every thrust, and Malachi felt secure in his mind's whispered *next time* and as he hungrily watched them dance.

"Oh God, I'm coming," she cried after a few minutes, her back arching, her thighs clamping around him.

"Yes," Malachi growled, his tail flicking around his hip to where they were joined, finding her swollen clit.

Joy's body locked up. Malachi held her to his straining length as she came, spasming around him. Stars burst behind his eyelids as he enjoyed the orgasm practically strangling his dick, his balls cramping.

When she relaxed, he resumed his movements, rutting into her like an animal, sweet little "*ah, ah, ah*"s escaping from Joy's mouth with every thrust.

"When you come, I want you to bite me," Joy gasped, the words leaving her lips like she was stating the time.

And Malachi was coming. He bent over her, slapping his hips into hers, his mouth working soundlessly at the intensity, his body shaking. His wings moved without his control, lifting them into the air for a brief moment, before they collapsed back onto the mattress.

"Holy shit," Joy whispered while Malachi tried to regain his senses, his face pressed into her neck. "Did you just fly? While you were *inside* me?" Her scent went smoky and hot.

Malachi nuzzled her throat, grinning, tucking her reaction away for later. "Well, my wings are certainly not just there for decoration."

Joy smacked his arm, but she was laughing. He leaned up on his elbows to look at her.

She bit her lower lip. "I missed you," she whispered.

Malachi's heart felt so fucking tender. "I missed you, too."

Joy's eyes were twinkling with happiness. Malachi leaned down, closing his eyes and pressing his forehead against hers.

"I'm—I'm not good at being vulnerable," he said, his voice so low she probably had to strain to hear him.

"Pot, meet kettle," Joy said.

He laughed, and opened his eyes. "I'm not good at being vulnerable," he repeated. "But I'd like to try with you."

Joy's eyes shone. "Me too." She cleared her throat when her voice came out hoarse. "Me too," she repeated, tilting her face up for a kiss.

Malachi kissed her, long and deep. He murmured against her mouth, "I wish to know—who is Joy, when she's not being murderous?"

Joy laughed. "Who is Malachi, when he's not making contracts?"

"I guess we have time now to find out," he said, not managing to keep the hope from his voice.

Joy's smile was so, so soft. "I guess we do."

EPILOGUE
One Year Later

Iyore was, unsurprisingly, a stunning bride. Joy had expected her to get a moment of cold feet, but all Iyore seemed to feel was joy. Joy's lips twitched at the entendre.

When Joy had summoned a demon to help her get rid of her rapist—permanently—she didn't think she'd turn into some kind of vigilante.

After she'd summoned Malachi the second time, and they'd spent a few blissful days talking and fucking and cuddling and basking in what felt suspiciously like a honeymoon glow, Joy had finally laid down her plan on how to get revenge against Iyore's uncle. Malachi had simply taken them into Iyore's dreamscape, manipulating it so the man in question appeared in the dream and they got his identity. After that, and a bit of digging, Joy completed the deed.

Iyore didn't seem to question it. After she'd announced it to Joy—"Heart attack," she'd said, her voice devoid of emotion, her face slack of all expression—Joy had taken her straight to Coldstone for a heap of ice-scream. Her best friend had cried, but Joy hadn't needed Malachi's supernatural senses to know they were happy tears. After their ice-cream—and pizza—they'd gone dancing with the rest of their friends, Malcom included, though only he and Joy knew the real reason for the impromptu outing.

After the funeral—which neither she, Iyore, nor Malcom had attended—the eagerness to get married suddenly lit a fire on Iyore's ass. She'd waited what she'd deemed an appropriate amount of time from the funeral, before she'd gone into the frenzy of preparing for her wedding.

Now, here they stood.

The groom's and bride's families were gathered in Iyore's family's ancestral home in the village of Araya. Most of them sat around the tacky velvet sofas, with the groom's family surrounding him on one side, the bride's on the other.

Iyore was standing in the middle of the circle, facing her future husband, who sat in one of the armchairs in front of her. They were both dressed in deep, traditional red velvet; Iyore in two wrappers tied around her frame, her afro combed and pinned to her head in an elaborate updo styled with coral beads. The same beads were wound around her neck, threaded with gold, along with her ears, wrists, and ankles. Malcom wore a cream kaftan and matching velvet wrappers of his own, his bald head hidden underneath a traditional velvet cap, a walking stick clutched tightly in one hand. He looked like a Prince.

"Iyore, my sweet daughter; we have all gathered here today because this man has said he wants to be your husband," her father said, his voice booming. "Do you accept his proposal?"

Iyore remained silent. They'd warned Malcom of the Isoko wedding traditions beforehand, but Joy could still see him sweating from here, which made her want to laugh.

"I will ask a second time," her father said. "Do you want this man to be your husband?"

Iyore remained silent. Beside her, Joy heard a soft, familiar chuckle that sent warmth blooming in her lower belly.

"He's shitting bricks," Malachi leaned over to whisper.

Joy bit back her laugh.

"I will ask a third time, and after this, I will not ask again. Do you want this man to be your husband?"

"Yes," Iyore said finally, decisively, to the cheers of the crowd and Malcom's immediate relief.

Joy dragged Malachi up to his feet along with everyone else. The bride was given a gourd filled with palmwine, and told to give the drink to her future husband. She did so, kneeling by his side, and the room burst into cheer when Malcom dutifully took a sip, then tipped the gourd for Iyore to drink as well, the action representing how they'd take care of each other during their marriage.

Afterward, she was gently led to the armchair beside Malcom's, their hands intertwined in the middle. The women began to clap and sing, everyone getting to their feet to dance.

They sang in Isoko; sweet songs praying for fruitfulness in their marriage and their lives and their happiness. Iyore and Malcom had eyes for no other, beaming and staring at each other, even though, according to tradition, they were both supposed to be stern and stoic until the ceremony ended. Iyore was supposed to then be danced out of the room, and Malcom was supposed to bring his gifts to the bride's family for their blessing and acceptance.

But fuck tradition, eh?

Once the prayer songs ended, the dancing songs began. The bride and groom stood. Some of the women ululated. Space was made in the middle of the room for them to have their first dance.

Joy cheered loudly. Iyore didn't hesitate to go down low and wind her hips, grinning widely and happily at her husband, while Malcom stared at her like it was the beginning of the rest of his life.

Joy's heart constricted tightly. She glanced at Malachi, who was taking it all in with the greedy excitement of a child. As the day to the wedding had drawn closer, it seemed he'd been more excited than the bride and groom themselves, desperately eager to witness the traditional wedding in all its wondrous, dramatic glory.

To everyone else, he was simply a tall, handsome, dark-skinned man with unnaturally long hair. They'd come up with an elaborate story that he'd come to Nigeria from abroad to do some work. He'd ended up enjoying his time here, and had decided to stay. He and Joy had met by chance, bumping into each other at a supermarket. They'd reached for the same carton of Indomie, hands brushing, and the rest, as they say, was history.

Joy's lips quirked as she recalled Iyore's squeals of how cute it was as she had narrated the false story, her hand tangled tightly in Malachi's. She remembered feeling a brief pang of something lost, wondering how it would have been if it had happened that way. Then she'd shoved melancholy aside. She wouldn't change what she had for the world, and not for something as ridiculous as "normality". She was a proud murderer of rapists; "normal" was no longer in her wheelhouse.

Now, Malachi was a regular part of their circle. He'd been so nervous at first, so afraid of fitting in; Joy's heart clenched hard with love for him.

When she turned back to face Iyore dancing with her husband, the love in her heart grew. Her heart raced as she thought of her own plans. She was supposed to enact them after the white wedding, but Joy didn't know if she could wait.

Marriage and kids and the whole shebang wasn't something she'd ever been interested in, but lifelong companionship? Now *that,* she had to admit, sounded pretty fucking good.

She glanced at Malachi again. He turned to look at her at the same time, his lips curving into a handsome grin. While he'd once let her see his "human" form just so she had an idea of what everyone else saw when they looked at him, to her eyes only, whether in public or in private, he remained himself—horns, wings, purple skin and all. Just as she preferred.

"Hi," Joy said dreamily, nonsensically.

"Hi." Malachi's grin widened. His feathers rustled, a sign that he was fighting the urge to preen. "You okay?" His left arm and wing went around her shoulders. His right hand came on top of hers, where she hadn't realised she'd been cracking her knuckles. Oops.

She stopped, then snuggled into his side. Her heart thumped hard against her ribs. "Yeah, I'm fine."

"Hm."

"What?" Joy said, but she was smiling, helplessly endeared by his antics. "I'm *fine*."

"Okay," Malachi said, lips twitching.

"I don't think I like your tone."

"What tone?"

Joy's eyes narrowed. They were in public, but she lifted onto her toes, pulling Malachi down to whisper in his ear, "Are you begging to be punished, demon boy?"

"What if I am, little tiger?" Malachi husked against her

throat.

Joy pressed a tiny kiss against the "v" at the base of his throat. He trembled, his arms wrapping around her.

"I love you," he said. He said it all the time—had confessed that he always said the words when he was thinking or feeling them. Which was, again, practically all the time.

She kissed him, uncaring of their audience; Nigerians really didn't do PDA, especially in front of other people, but Joy didn't care. She imagined how Malachi might react when she enacted her plan, and it filled her stomach immediately with butterflies because she knew—she just *knew* what his response would be.

God. Joy wasn't going to wait. Fuck waiting until after the white wedding, even though that was literally in two days.

She wanted Malachi now, and she intended to have him. Now, and forever.

Joy was hiding something. It wasn't just in the shifty edge to her scent, or the rapid thump of her heartbeat; it was the way she kept biting her lower lip and glancing at him from the corner of her eye like he wouldn't notice; the way she kept cracking her knuckles, one by one, over and over again until he'd had to place his hand on top of hers to make her stop.

After the dancing and spraying of money, they all ate, the elders in the bride's family accepted the gifts brought from the groom's family, broke some kola nuts in half and recited more prayers, then the bride and groom were danced out of the house.

Joy disappeared to the bathroom at some point. When

she returned, she was practically glowing, trembling with barely concealed excitement. Like the rest of the women, she was dressed in traditional Isoko attire; an intricately wrapped headscarf around her head that resembled the shape of a rose, a glittery pale blue blouse made with fine lace and chiffon, and dark purple velvet wrappers with silvery designs at the bottom hems. In her hand, she held a small, silver clutch.

She came up to him, beaming.

"I love you," Malachi couldn't help but say, because he did. He wondered if she'd ever tire of him blurting it out at every moment, but every single time, she reacted like it was the first time.

"I love you, too," she said, still vibrating.

Malachi held out his arm, smiling fondly. "Are you ready?"

She slid her fingers into the dip of his elbow. "Yes."

They walked a bit aways from the crowd before Malachi let them morph through the aether, appearing in Joy's flat where they usually spent most of their time. His castle in Mmuo had become some kind of home away from home, where they went when they wanted to be completely shut out from the rest of the world, doing nothing but making love, hand-feeding each other, and devouring his book and film library.

Just as they appeared in the flat, Malachi's phone vibrated with a text. He raised an eyebrow when he saw the message.

"Klaus needs me for something," he said, looking at Joy.

"Okay," Joy said innocently.

Malachi's second eyebrow joined the first. "No protests about the time? Or how we've just come from a wedding and we're exhausted and whatever they have to say to me can wait until tomorrow?"

"Nope. You go on ahead," Joy said cheerfully. "Are you

hungry? I can order something for when you get back."

Malachi's eyes narrowed. "I'm onto you."

"Sure," Joy drawled.

Sometimes, Malachi almost couldn't stand how much he loved her.

"Fine. I'm going. I love you."

"Love you, too! Take your time!"

"Okay, now I *know* you're up to something."

"Uh-huh." Joy laughed, pecking him quick and firm on his lips. "Bye-bye, now."

The moment Malachi disappeared, Joy called her aunt.

"I'm doing it tonight," she said without preamble.

"Ahn, ahn, not even a "hello, Aunty, good evening"?"

Joy blushed. "Sorry. Good evening, Aunty."

"Much better." Aunty Paloma sounded amused. "And yeah? Tonight, eh? How are you feeling?"

"Nervous." She swallowed hard. "Scared. Just a little bit."

"I know the feeling. I won't tell you not to be scared because that's pointless. But I will say: it's going to be totally fucking worth it."

Joy grinned wide. If Aunty Paloma was cursing, then she really meant that shit. Joy said her goodbyes, thanked her aunt for her support, and ended the call.

She squared her shoulders. This was a little more permanent than a ring, but Joy wasn't the type to do things halfway. If she was in, she was all in.

Klaus was even bigger than Malachi, though where Malachi was taut with muscle, Klaus was soft and round all over. Joy's friends were nice, but there was just something about having a friend like Klaus, someone who knew intimately about how life in hell could be.

Unlike Malachi, Klaus had come from a laxer sect. They were also decades older than Malachi, and had grown tired of all the politics and rules and laws constricting nicquiris back in hell. Most Sovereigns were nicquiris themselves, and in order to maintain their power, they had the tendency to snip any up-and-coming nicquiris in the bud.

When Klaus had realised they were now considered powerful enough to be a threat to the Sovereign nicquiris, and was thus being hunted by sentries, they'd run to earth, and had incidentally, at the same time, fallen right into Paloma's arms. They'd been here ever since.

"What's all this about?" Malachi asked as he appeared through the aether and into the park in the centre of the small community Klaus lived in with their human.

"Hello." Klaus turned to face him, a small smile on their full lips. Like Malachi, Klaus had deep, plum skin, though their shade was a touch lighter than Malachi's. Their afro was a short inch off their scalp, their wings wider and fluffier. Their horns were larger as well, though the one on the right was broken right at the curve.

"You have nothing to say to me, do you?" Malachi asked dryly.

Klaus's lips twitched. "I do not."

Malachi sighed heavily. "We may as well sit."

Klaus grinned. "Good man."

"Sure I can't persuade you to tell me what's going on?"

"You cannot."

Malachi sighed.

Klaus began to talk about their garden—their fucking

garden, for fuck's sake, and it felt like an eternity but must only have been thirty minutes when Malachi felt a familiar tug behind his ribs.

He frowned, rubbing at his chest. He and Joy didn't currently have a contract, so why was—

Oh. *Oh.*

Malachi stood. Klaus did as well. Malachi, despite himself, was blushing. Joy "summoning" him had kind of become foreplay for them.

Malachi cleared his throat. "Well. Good luck with your, um, plants."

"Good luck with your lady."

Malachi blushed. He disappeared through the aether, following the tug in his heart and appearing again to find Joy kneeling in the middle of a summoning rune drawn with white chalk.

She wasn't wearing her usual bathrobe. Instead, she was dressed in velvet wrappers and coral beads. Malachi blinked, staring at her. Faintly, he realised his heart had begun to race.

The clothing didn't mean anything; they weren't only worn by brides on their wedding days. Besides, Joy had mentioned not being interested in the human concept of marriage, which Malachi would never admit had been slightly disappointing. Not that he cared that much, either; it would have just been nice to be that to each other. To exchange vows. Promise themselves to the other.

Joy stood. She was vibrating with energy. Malachi found himself vibrating too, helplessly ensnared by her.

"I'm here to make a deal," she began, at the same time that he said, "I love you."

Joy grinned, wide and happy and carefree, her scent like sunshine on flowers. "I love you, too. Now, please respond. I said I'm here to make a deal."

Malachi laughed. "That much is obvious." She didn't

reek of bloodthirst, so he didn't mention it, saying instead, "Why have you summoned me, pretty tiger?"

At this point, Joy grew nervous, fiddling with the edges of her wrapper. She licked her painted lips. Malachi's stomach was twisting all over itself. A part of him felt like it knew what was going on, though Malachi's conscious mind downright refused to put two and two together.

"I'm here because ... I want to ... own someone. And I want them to own me."

Malachi's body went still. The aware thing in the back of his mind was screaming, but he wasn't listening. That couldn't be it. Surely—no.

"You haven't brought a sacrifice." The words left his lips by rote.

And Joy smiled one of the rarer smiles—one she held for Malachi and Malachi alone.

"I offer you my soul."

Malachi thought he blacked out for a moment. He swallowed the saliva pooling in his mouth. "I'm sorry, what?"

"My soul, Malachi," Joy whispered, her dark eyes shining with laughter—with *joy*. "It's yours to take."

Malachi reached into her circle for her. She came eagerly, pressing up against his chest, her breaths speeding.

"Joy." He was trembling.

"Yes?" she answered sweetly.

Malachi swallowed again. "I—Joy. This is—"

"More permanent than marriage." Her expression softened; her eyes darkened. "I know."

Malachi kissed her, hard and deep. "Yes," he rasped. "*Yes*."

He moved on impulse. His hand twisted through the air, and a piece of paper formed into his grasp, sparking with embers that slowly burned off, leaving the edges of the paper dark and scarred.

He pressed it to Joy's hand; the lump in his throat seemed to have found itself a home right there.

"My name," he whispered. "My *True* Name."

Joy's eyes blew wide. She yanked him down, kissing him hard.

"I love you," she whispered. "I love you so much." She took the piece of paper. She didn't even look at it, folding it instead into a neat little square. Her smile was so full of love Malachi didn't know how he could stand it. "You'll always be Malachi to me." Her scent went smoky; possessive. "But this name is mine, yeah?"

Fuck. "Yes. I love you."

Joy's eyes twinkled. "Can you—?" She gestured at the paper.

Even without a bond, Malachi instinctively knew what she wanted. He waved his hand again, and the paper morphed, changing form and shape and matter until it had turned into a small, silver ring.

Joy slid it onto her ring finger, then she yanked Malachi down and kissed him again, over and over and over.

"Say the vow," Malachi said desperately against her mouth, almost shaking with it.

"Igris, entis, untis, represe."

The bond lit up like a fire behind his chest, bright and painful and startling. Joy laughed, her right hand fluttering up to her chest; she could feel it, too.

They slammed into each other, kissing hard. They stumbled to the bed, landing on top of it, still kissing. Malachi got rid of their clothes with a flick of his wrist.

"Fuck." Joy gasped, squirming on top of him. "It's so hot when you do that."

"I know," he said, grinning, eyes glittering.

"Shut up and kiss me."

They got lost in each other's lips. Joy rocked on top of

him, thighs spread, her cunt gliding along the length of his dick, growing warmer and wetter the longer they kissed. It was so sexy how arousing she found kissing, which made him find it arousing in turn.

When she sat up, reaching for his dick, he stopped her, a flush in his cheeks.

"I want you inside me," he whispered.

Joy practically melted. "Of course, darling," she murmured.

Another flick of his wrist, and the lube and her dick— she'd had him make a magical one for her in the same shade of his skin; she'd thought it was fitting, which made Malachi laugh—appeared by her bent knee. She picked up the lube and adjusted her position, moving until she was kneeling on the bed, his thighs spread over her lap. She drenched her hand in sticky wetness, then pressed her fingers against his rim.

Malachi moaned, arching into her touch. It shouldn't be different, he knew, but to him it was. When Joy pushed her fingers into him, her eyes locked on his, it shouldn't have made Malachi burn; it shouldn't have made him feel—every single time—like he was being claimed in the most intimate way possible.

"Okay?" she whispered, thrusting three fingers into him at once, knowing he could take it.

"I love you," he moaned, gripping the sheets, tears filling his eyes.

Joy smiled, her eyes filled with emotion. "I love you, too."

Malachi's soft sighs and moans were the loudest sounds in the room, over the lewd, wet thrusts of her fingers inside him. His dick was straining, flushed dark and leaking trails of white onto his belly.

Joy curled her fingers. Malachi's hips jolted, his dick pulsing.

"Please." He was close already, but he wanted to come with her inside him.

"Yeah? Are you ready for me, big boy?"

He met her eyes, his own heavy-lidded. "Fuck me. Please."

Joy groaned, sliding her fingers out with a wet squelch. She pressed the flat end of the dick between her legs, groaning, thick thighs shaking as the magic took hold, wrapping around her cunt and sucking at her clit like a mouth.

"Jesus," she gasped, curling in on herself for a moment as the sensations wrecked her like they did every time. "Holy fucking shit."

Her right hand went underneath his thigh, lifting his left leg higher, the other holding her dick and aiming it at his entrance.

"I love you," she said, then thrust into him.

Malachi arched with a sharp cry. His wings flared wide behind him. Joy didn't give him a moment to adjust, rocking into him immediately, her hands gripping his thighs, her hips rolling sexily.

"Fuck, Joy. I love you. I love you." She felt so good inside him, filling him up like this; he never wanted it to end.

"Fuck." Joy panted, pumping into him harder, faster, her hips tilted at the perfect angle that had the head of her length hitting the right spot over and over again. Malachi fisted the sheets, crying out each time she filled him.

"Touch yourself for me, darling," she commanded. "Let me see you come."

Malachi whimpered. The moment he had a hand on himself, he was gone, crying out and coming all over his fist, clenching greedily around the hardness inside him.

Joy fell on top of him, kissing him harshly as her thrusts lost all sense of rhythm. "Who do you belong to?" she asked between kisses, her hands moving up to grip his horns, her eyes burning.

"You," Malachi said with all the conviction he felt, gasping with each stuttered grind into him, his arms wrapping around her. "Oh fuck—you, you, you."

"You're *mine*." She growled as she came, sobbing on top of him, her hips grinding hard into him, riding the orgasm out.

Her spoken claim made the bond in his chest thrum hard, and Malachi cried out as he lost control, his wings beating hard, lifting them high off the mattress. His body locked up as he experienced a mirroring orgasm, his dick aching with it.

Joy laughed when they landed back on the mattress with an undignified thump. She pressed a kiss into his jaw, melting on top of him, struggling to catch her breath.

"And I'm yours." She sighed. In a moment, Malachi knew she would be fast asleep.

He smiled as he closed his eyes, his arms tightening around her. It felt good to be home.

Acknowledgements

SWEET VENGEANCE was honestly not supposed to happen; at least, not for a few years. I've always wanted to write a monster/demon romance, and when I finally got the idea of a murderous woman hellbent on cold, hard revenge summoning a demon to help her get away with murder, the idea literally refused to leave me alone until I sat down and just had to write it. Thank you, ADHD brain.

First of all, as always, I'd like to thank my readers on patreon: thank you all so, so much for your support over the past few years. It has meant absolutely everything.

Thank you so much to my family; it took me literal weeks to illustrate this cover (thanks again, ADHD-perfectionist brain), and all of you—Mummy, Mano, Zino, and Bruno— were there with me when I tore my hair out in frustration; you encouraged me to press publish despite me wanting to take everything going wrong as a "sign" that maybe this book wasn't meant to be. Thank you for staying by my side, for reminding me that setbacks happen, and, as Zino repeated often enough, that "You have to start from somewhere."

And to you, reader, thank you so much for taking the chance to buy SWEET VENGEANCE, and helping me take one step closer to fulfilling my dream of becoming a self-sufficient, self-published author.

I hope you enjoyed the ride.

ALSO BY VIANO ONIOMOH

For more books filled with swoony romance and BIPOC LGBTQ+ characters, check out Viano's other books:

In CUPID CALLING, Ejiro and Obiora are competing alongside twenty-eight other bachelors for the heart of one bachelorette. They shouldn't be falling for each other.

In FRAGMENTS OF A FALLEN STAR, Moira Karl-Fisher journeys across the sea to find the missing pages of a spell to turn back time.

In THE AURORA CIRCUS, a spirit's plea for help leads Ember Quinn to the magical world of *The Aurora Circus*.

Exclusive Content on Patreon

Interested in more content? For as little as $3/month, you get access to over 400,000+ words worth of full-length novels, novellas, and short stories, along with Behind The Scenes content, early cover reveals, early ebook releases, signed physical copies, exclusive merch, and more!

Subscribe to Viano's Newsletter

Subscribe to Viano's Newsletter for exclusive perks, early cover reveals, giveaways and more, and be the first to get the latest updates about Viano and her work.

About the Author

Viano Oniomoh is a passionate reader and writer, who was born and raised in Nigeria. She spends fifty percent of her time writing, forty percent reading, and the other ten listening to BTS. She may or may not use magic to get everything else in her life done. She also has no idea how to write about herself in the third person.

Stay in touch with Viano via her social media pages linked below, or alternatively, you can contact her via her website at vianooniomoh.com

Lightning Source UK Ltd.
Milton Keynes UK
UKHW041459200223
417327UK00003B/181

9 798375 809328